Romance Is Like That

Liian Varus

Copyright © 2025 Liian Varus

All rights reserved.

ISBN: 9798282271386

IN LOVING MEMORY OF FAX MACHINE.

THE ITINERARY

1	Dave, Caroline & That Bitch Brenda	Pg #1
2	No Teddy Bear Picnic	Pg #8
3	Business & Brenda Are Villains	Pg #16
4	Love Is Not A Triforce	Pg #27
5	Everything Bagel With Herbs & Garlic Cream Cheese	Pg #36
6	Mortimer's Plan	Pg #45
7	Orgasm & The Ham Sandwich	Pg #54
8	Out Of Business	Pg #65
9	Blub	Pg #74
10	The Sex	Pg #85

DAVE, CAROLINE & THAT BITCH BRENDA

It's Halloween night, and there she is — Caroline, a thirty-three-year-old girl donning a yellow banana costume, a full-fledged woman by most cultural standards, lying down so still as if she's superimposed to the red velvet chaise that makes people think she's rich. Truth is, she owns a modest condo in a town you've probably heard of before; the chaise came with the place.

Circling back. There she is, getting lost in Dave's one brown eye and one blue eye. His eyes are two different colours. Dave is staring in return. Caroline's eyes are aphid green, smiling intently with excitement like she's about to solve a Rubik's Cube for the first time. Dave smiles too because he also loves Rubik's Cubes. Their chemistry is more than undeniable — it's nonrefundable. Dave leans towards her and kisses her with his mouth. She accepts it, ready to give in to her sexual desires. Dave, bashfully with clammy fingers, peels off Caroline's costume imported from South America, exposing her blouse. Button by button, one by one, they pop off, revealing not one nipple, but two nipples. Dave, all the while grinning like a degenerate child because it reminds him of Tiddlywinks. There's no doubt — it was time to monkey around.

After thirty-three years, sex would be theirs. Just as Caroline is giving Dave consent for him to be a top, his phone rings. It's his business calling. Dave looks at Caroline. Caroline looks at Dave, nodding affirmatively, understanding how much Dave loves doing business.

Dave stands up and picks up the phone. "Hello. This is Dave." Dave hangs up the phone; a long frown tells Caroline she could have worn a bra today. "I have to go. It's business. They need me to come into the office to do some business for the business."

Caroline is disappointed, but she knows it's important. The exploration of their genitals would have to wait.

Dave kisses her on the forehead. "Sorry, it's business."

"I know. It's okay. I'll get over it. I'm supportive because romance is like that," she says reassuringly.

Dave puts on his realistic astronaut helmet and pretends to moonwalk out the door. Caroline laughs. Dave always has a way of making her feel warm feelings.

They're the bestest of friends. Dave and Caroline have had this special bond since they've known each other as fetuses. Both are thirty-three, both with the exact same birthdate; they were even born in the same shit town, same underfunded hospital. What brought them together, though, was tragedy. Dave's parents died in a freak chuckwagon accident. He had to be surgically removed from his dead mother. Sorry. That joke was premature.

In a crazy universe, Caroline's parents also died in a freak chuckwagon accident, and she too had to be medically extracted like Dave. So many similarities. No wonder they grew so close, fell so madly in love.

Dave and Caroline's parents were bitter rivals, racing for two different teams. Distracted by blind hatred for each other, they didn't see the cliffside, riding straight off it and into the salty ocean, where they and their horses were then nautically struck by a cruise liner. That day, no one was having fun. I know – I'm also surprised Dave and Caroline survived, and I'm the one who's writing the story.

It's one in the morning, and Dave is back at the office, tirelessly working away at a pile of business sitting at his business desk. Despite it being four hours past Dave's bedtime, Dave plugs away. He knows if he wants his business to succeed at business, he needs to finish all this business. Although Dave dreams that his business will be the world's best business at business one day, he can't stop thinking about Caroline and how he should be there, taking off the rest of her clothes. Albeit the insatiable yearning to see what she looks like below her navel, he continues tackling the mountain of paperwork for his business. Dave is a hard worker.

Back at the condo, Caroline is on the phone, experiencing

sad feelings. She's talking to her not-so-best friend, Brenda. Brenda is upset, as most Brendas are. She doesn't like how Dave constantly chooses business over her best friend, Caroline. Brenda thinks Caroline tells people they're best friends. Brenda is delusional and lonely as fuck.

"You don't deserve to be treated like a thrift shop item. You don't deserve to be cast aside every time Dave needs to do business. You should be his first prime example of love," Brenda scolds. On all accounts, Brenda is a fucking bitch.

"He does love me though. Of course, it would be nice to be his priority and outrank business, and I believe one day I'll get there, but for now, it is what it is. I love him and he loves me. That's what matters," Caroline sniffles, wiping away the wayward snot running out of her nose with one of her banana arms.

Brenda grits her teeth, wanting to say something a bitch would say, but reminds herself that Caroline is her best friend, even though she's an insane person living in a goddamn fantasy world. Man, fuck Brenda.

"Listen. Fine. I support the decision your brain and heart have collaborated on. I hope he comes around and wants to see what you look like below your navel someday," says Brenda, pretending to give a shit, secretly wishing Dave would die so she can ruin Caroline's life all by herself.

Caroline is aware that Brenda isn't Dave's biggest fan, but if anything, she feels sorry for her. So she politely says, "Thank you." She changes the subject because Brenda doesn't understand romance is like that. "Hey, Brenda, remember last year when you lost your right foot to frostbite because Jeff at work accidentally locked you inside an industrial freezer for eight hours?"

Brenda loosens her orangutan teeth and opens her stupid mouth. "Yeah, that Jeff is so clumsy sometimes."

Caroline dries her eyes as her tear ducts swell with joy water. But what Brenda doesn't realize is that Jeff hates her guts. The fact she kept stealing his utility knife without asking, her insufferable personality and reeking of Pacific halibut eggs decomposing inside a vat of blue cheese every day – well, he couldn't take it anymore; he snapped. Unfortunately, my dear reader, Brenda unknowingly survived a murder attempt. However, because Jeff tried eliminating her, he was promoted to warehouse supervisor. His manager and coworkers knew, appreciated what he tried to do for them. Unlike Brenda, Jeff is a great human being.

As the conversation grows silently awkward, because that bitch Brenda never knows when it's her cue to fuck off, Caroline intervenes. "Brenda, it's late. I need to get some sleep. Dave and I have a picnic planned later today, but please feel free to call at another inconvenient time for me that works for you."

"A picnic?! A PICNIC?! It's going to be -33 degrees! It's practically winter outside?!" glarps Brenda, because she's a jealous bitch.

Caroline replies calmly, "Brenda, Brenda, it's okay. You've never been loved by anyone and probably never will, but I promise romance is like that. Dave and I are going to enjoy creating more memories for us. I'm sorry you won't ever know what that's like. Have a good night."

Brenda hangs up first. She's unnecessarily competitive about everything. "I'm so glad Caroline and I are the bestest of friends. She's lucky to have me in her life," bragging, turning to her fifteen-year-old cat, who can't wait to die already. Cheddar too has also had enough of Brenda's shit. Every day he regrets Brenda finding him dying on the side of the road. At first, he was excited, but it wasn't long 'til he knew the universe had catfished him. He plays back that moment countlessly – if only he could have crawled far enough into that bush to die, maybe then she wouldn't have seen him.

"I should have died. I deserve better than this," Cheddar meows to himself, finishing taking a shit in Brenda's left neon green Croc. Every day Cheddar dreams of smothering Brenda with a pillow in her sleep. Hey, let's go check in on Dave.

"I am so glad my business is doing lots and lots of business, but sometimes I wish business would slow down a bit, so I can have a chance to see what Caroline looks like below her navel. Gosh, I love her." Dave ruffles through paperwork, wondering if that day will ever come.

As the sun peeks up over the horizon, Dave panics. He forgot about his picnic date. Finding the important document that confirms his business is on the correct trajectory toward positive business practices, he grabs his fancy leather briefcase and a bottle of sparkling water from his mini business fridge, which is perfectly placed with the label facing forward. Because if this book ever gets turned into a movie, it would make for a great product placement shot. Dave takes a swig. "Yum," smacking his lips, confirming to future potential brands – the sparkling water successfully quenched his thirst. He heads out the door for home, to catch a few hours of sleep before his picnic date with Caroline.

It's eight in the morning and Caroline's alarm informs her she has to open her eyes and start a whole day of adulting. She smiles like a clown waking up from a melatonin coma. "I can't wait to see Dave! I hope he brings fresh produce for our special picnic! Do you think he'll bring guava, Mortimer? I love guava!" Caroline shrieks with excitement. Mortimer doesn't reply because he's a fucking goldfish.

Caroline is a sweet girl, but sometimes she lives her life like she's living in a Disney movie. It's not healthy. Caroline jumps into the shower, making sure her body smells like lavender soap and not night sweats. As she soaps her legs with a foam bouquet of flower-scented body wash, she's confident this is the day – Dave will see what she looks like below her navel. She gets the jitters. Caroline stops lathering. Her body is telling her to do something to it that she doesn't have time for. Caroline doesn't bother washing her hair. The last thing she needs is an orgasm that makes her weak in the knees, causing her to slip in the shower, hitting her head against the edge of the tub and ruining this soon-to-be magic moment. She was not going to risk a cumcussion, not today. Yes. Cumcussion. I know what I said. Anyway, I've never seen a woman get ready for a date before, so if you're a woman or someone who has seen that happen – she's doing all those things exceptionally well. Caroline makes sure to feed Mortimer before she goes, because she knows starving a defenceless animal to death is wrong, grabs a banana muffin from the counter, and throws on her red peacoat and yellow sandals. What's she wearing to her picnic date? I don't know. I'd imagine some sort of floral dress. Women are like that. Honestly, who fucking cares? "Goodbye Mortimer, my special little guy, have a great day," blowing him a smoochy kiss.

"Blub, blub," Mortimer doing the best he can as a registered emotional support Carassius auratus. He goes back to mouthing bubbles in his favourite corner of his tank.

Caroline leaves.

Dreaming about reigning over the Kingdom of Business, and how all his loyal subjects adore his business ethics and his efficiency of working around the gossip at the royal watercooler, Dave is unaware he forgot to set his alarm. Unbeknownst to him, he's an hour and thirteen minutes late. If he doesn't wake soon, this could be the final straw that... Oh, never mind, he's up. Dave rubs his eyes, squints over to his alarm clock and panics. There are many times when Caroline forgave Dave for his ungentlemanly inadequacies because romance is like that, but the feeling in Dave's gut is telling him if he doesn't get there soon, he could lose her forever. Fortunately for Dave, he's still wearing his business suit. That saved him some precious time. The business suit is blue. He hastily but thoroughly brushes his teeth. Dave believes gingivitis can bankrupt a business with one smile. Dave's teeth sparkle like a LiteBrite with only white pegs. Dave slips on his fancy loafers he got on super sale at a shoe outlet store last year. They're brown.

"Brenda's a bitch. Brenda's a goddamn fucking bitch. Bitch. Bitch. Bitch. Bitch." Dave smiles as his blue-and-yellow macaw Fax Machine reminds him that Brenda is indeed a bitch.

Dave rushes out the door. If he hurries, he can still make it; there's a chance Caroline will show him what she looks like below her navel. His only hope is that Caroline doesn't forget romance is like that. On his electric bike in three feet of snow, he dangerously swerves all over the road, committing minor bylaw infractions, heading to their special picnic spot.

Back at its evil lair — Dave's office, Business methodically flips a Rolodex, memorizing hundreds of important numbers for Dave to call later with regards to business expansion and ventures. Business is confident Dave is soon going to have a lot more free time. Sorry. The B in Business will sometimes be capitalized now because I've decided I want Business manifested into a main villain character for the story. Could it be? Did Business finally destroy Dave and Caroline's relationship with too much business? Will Dave make it to the picnic on time? With their love hanging in the balance, there's only one way to find out — reading beyond this point. No need to sigh. You don't have to. It's merely a suggestion. No one has a gun pointed at your head. You can put the book down. It's fine. Jesus.

NO TEDDY BEAR PICNIC

Three hours later Dave finally arrives at their special picnic spot. Pulling up he can see Caroline standing by a tree missing leaves. They're on the snowy ground because the tree is deciduous and it's November. From a hill, you can see the river slowly moving past the city. It's reminiscent of every romantic movie filmed in New York, but it's not New York because there are no hills in New York. Dave gets off his electric bike and trudges through three feet of snow toward Caroline, as her floral dress gently blows in the winter breeze almost as if it were frozen in time. Winter came early. Dave and Caroline did not pay attention to the weather report beforehand. He smiles as he makes his way towards her.

"Man, she looks lovely," Dave swooning at the back of her head and the ornate design of her dress fabric because he can't see her face from where he's standing. Hypnotized by her long brown hair whisking out like a Harlequin romance novel love interest, he approaches her and stands at her side. Probably the left side. "Sorry, I'm late, my love. The 4x4 setting on my electric bike wasn't working. How are you?" bending over, huffing, trying to catch his breath, wishing he had purchased those futuristic carbon fibre snowshoes on Amazon last week. Then something catches his eye; he sees a zoo on the other side of the river. "Hey, do you think they have bears?" he asks, completely unaware that particular zoo went into foreclosure thirty years ago. "Seems pretty quiet. Oh, what am I thinking? Duh. I'm silly. It's November; the bears are hibernating. That's okay, they deserve it. We should go there in the spring. I bet they'll have cubs. Would you like that?"

Caroline doesn't reply.

"Caroline? Caroline?" Dave inquires worryingly, concerned about the lack of communication between them.

Dave steps in front of her. Dave lets out a gasp of shock. Caroline has been in the cold for so long, she looks like a live-action Jack Torrance replica doll. Dave takes one last hopeful glance behind him, to make sure the zoo doesn't have any bears roaming about. Peering intently from the distance he felt confident enough that indeed the bears must be asleep for the premature winter.

Dave turns his attention back to Caroline. "I don't think the bears are out so don't be disheartened, but you look cold. Oh, my love, why didn't you wear a dress with sleeves?" Dave chuckles to ease the tension, trying to make Caroline feel comfortable about her poor wardrobe choices. Last thing Dave wants is to embarrass Caroline on their special picnic date. "Hey, where is the picnic basket?" Dave bobbing his head around the surroundings like an overly curious and manic cockatoo. "Sweetie, you forgot it, didn't you? That's okay. At least we're here together. Nothing could make this moment more memorable. You're all I need. Although, a ham sandwich would have been nice." Dave forgives her unequivocally because romance is like that. Dave inquisitively checks behind him again. "Yeah, those huggable bears are not coming out," Dave muttering defeatedly, feeling bummed about the lost opportunity for him and Caroline to have their very own teddy bear picnic. "Alright, let's get you out of here. We need to get you warmed up." Dave gives her a long passionate kiss. In an instant, the ice melded to Caroline's body begins to melt like a snowwoman fantasizing about receiving oral from The Human Torch or when Brenda's cold heart thaws for a second because someone offers her the rest of their lunch.

"Where... Where am I?" Caroline asks, shivering like a lost geriatric patient aimlessly wandering about in a winter wonderland.

"We're at our special picnic spot where we were going to create extra memories," replies Dave. "My sweetener, why are you barefooted? Where's your coat? Where the tarnation is your car?" Dave poorly trying to hide the fact the author forgot he mentioned Caroline left wearing a red peacoat and sandals. I'll explain the whereabouts of the car in a second.

"I... I... I... don't know," says Caroline, chittering her teeth like chattering teeth.

Dave scours the area with his 20/20 vision because he's holding Caroline tight, trying to warm her body up to room temperature. He then sees her non-electric car upside down at the bottom of the embankment. The car is probably a red sedan. Well, that's how I'm imagining it. Caroline works for a marketing firm that deals with children dying from cancer, so the car has to be something practical. Anything fancier than that, then she would probably come off as an insensitive bitch and that's not her style. She's a sweetheart.

"I'm getting you out of here," Dave proclaims heroically. Scanning the area with precision, pretending he's a technologically advanced metal robot from the future who has power vision, he notices a toboggan leaning against the deciduous tree Caroline almost died at. "I got an idea!" Dave grabs the toboggan and lays it down. Caroline's lips twinkle as he puts her on it. She feels blessed that she has a man who loves her undeniably despite the fact she forgot to bring the picnic basket and didn't wear a dress with sleeves on such a cold day. She felt like a Disney princess, and as we all know by now, that's Caroline's kink.

"Don't worry about your red sedan. I'll have business take care of it and any damages. I've got you," Dave tells her assertively.

Caroline hates to admit it, but sometimes Dave's business has its perks but still doesn't change her irritable feelings about how often it impedes Dave from seeing what she looks like below her navel. She loves Dave with her whole heart. Would be nice to love him with her vagina too for once. If you ask Dave now, he would agree.

Holding onto the toboggan's yellow rope, he hops onto his electric bike and starts pulling Caroline behind him, switching back and forth between pedalling with manual labour and electricity – Dave realizing perhaps this mode of transportation isn't ideal for winter driving and isn't certain which would be less detrimental to their health. Dave is scared, but Dave also made the mistake of coming off as a fucking hero, so he has to play it through. If he gave up, Caroline might not see him how he's envisioning himself. He's going to get her home because that's what heroes do. There is still a chance to save their special picnic date and universe willing, be able to see what Caroline looks like below her navel.

"WEEEEEEEEEEEEEE! What fun!" Caroline screams with excitement.

Dave laughs cordially, aloud. He loves it when Caroline expresses happy feelings. It sets his world ablaze. Her smile is as infectious as Brenda's HSV-1. You don't want to know.

Dave is the luckiest man in the world. Caroline is the luckiest woman in the world. You're jealous. I get it. So am I – and I'm married. Well, not anymore. We're separated but are still living together, so now I'm miserable without any of the sex benefits.

Dave slams on the brakes. Caroline's body immediately thrusts against the back tire of his electric bike. "Got you!" Dave slapping his knee in hysterics. Dave always has the best pranks.

Caroline brushes off the snow, wagging her finger at Dave jokingly, yet sternly, "Oh, I'll get you back for that. Wait and see, Mister."

Dave gets off his electric bike. "We're here," helping Caroline up to her feet. "Let's get you inside your condo. I'll run you a hot bath, then I'll call business to pull some business strings to get your car towed and fixed up. I'll put the bill on my business' business account. Don't worry, you'll have your red sedan back in no time."

As much as Caroline isn't too fond of business, she does appreciate Dave is willing to do that for her and can because he has a profitable business. As they walk inside, Caroline snuggles up close to Dave. Although disappointed that she didn't get a chance to explode her taste buds with the holy flavours of a guava at their picnic, her hormones are enticed by the idea of Dave seeing what she looks like below her navel. She couldn't wait to get fully dethawed and pounce on him with the ferocity of a wild jungle cat.

"Dave thinks he knows business but wait until he gets a load of my business. I'm going to show him my CEOh face," giggling to herself.

As they head up the stairs towards her condo on the 33rd floor, Dave is thrilled to have the love of his life in his arms, but a sadness is lingering – Dave can't get over not being able to see any bears today. "Life is cruel. I want justice," says Dave vengefully to himself. He contemplates breaking into the zoo so he can see them do bear things, but when Dave looks into Caroline's eyes, he settles down. He knows he has saved the day. He's a goddamn hero and knows an opportunity to see what Caroline looks like below her navel is a real possibility. "To hell with those bears. I'm going to get mine," he says to himself in a sort of Chad way.

This isn't like Dave at all, but waiting thirty-three years to Cat's Cradle body parts with someone is a long time. A feral urge is physically changing his DNA. Dave is adamant that Caroline is going to get the humping she deserves, wants. Unlocking the door to her condo on the 61st floor, similar to the way Dave unlocked her heart all those years ago, they walk inside.

"BLUB! BLUB!" Mortimer instantly loses his shit at the sight of Dave. He loves Caroline. But Dave – HE FUCKING LOVES DAVE! Mortimer excitingly spins in his bowl, jumping out and into the water, just screaming at the top of his gills. "BLUB! BLUB!" That's fish for 'Dave.' Not confident if I used quotations correctly there, but you'll get over it.

As Dave sits Caroline on the couch, he looks over to see Mortimer fan basing his tiny body for him. "Hey Mortimer, little buddy," greeting Mortimer with a wink and a casually cool finger gun as he walks upstairs to the bathroom to run Caroline a hot bath. Yes, Caroline's condo has two floors, because she's smart with her money. Mortimer just fucking dies. He loves Dave so much. The only thing Mortimer wants in his entire life is for Caroline and Dave to get married, so Dave can be his new dad. His real dad is nothing but a dead bait.

Dave runs the tub hot enough to stimulate the senses of a lobster, adds some Epsom salts and five big spurts of citrusy bubble bath. Just as Dave is about to light a cinnamon raisin candle, out of the blue 'Takin' Care Of Business' begins rocking out from his pants pocket. His heart sinks. It's business. At first, Dave is excited, because if he doesn't keep up with his business, then he won't have any business to do for his business anymore. The excitement doesn't last long – realizing it means he has to leave is giving him painful feelings. Caroline and Dave are having such an amazing day even though Dave never got to see any bears. Not only that, but despite me, forgetting to mention how severe the sexual tension is from sexual innuendos they shared between each other on the way back to Caroline's condo, it felt like today was the day the sex was going to be theirs. Surprisingly, he let his cell phone ring a whole three times before answering. Dave may be the one answering the phone, but he knows in his heart he has made the wrong call. How is he going to break the news to Caroline? She'll be devastated. I didn't bother with the phone call dialogue between Dave and his business because I figured it was too boring.

"Was that business?!" yells Caroline from the living room. Not yelling because she's mad, but since the tub is running, she wants to make sure Dave can hear how unhappy she is.

Dave turns off the water. It's probably full enough. Anyway, Dave is going through some major guilty feelings right now. Let me exploit them. "It was. I have to do business in thirty minutes," Dave replies shamefully.

Caroline sheds a tear. Her vagina cries harder. Dave feels like a big asshole. Dave has a lot of ME work to do. He has to try and make this correct with some more promises he can't keep. He has to do something.

"BLUB! BLUB!" Mortimer losing his absolute shit over the site of Dave as he walks down the stairs and into the living room.

Dave looks at Mortimer and motions for him to settle. His

timing is inappropriate for the melancholic uprising his heart is battling but gave him the tiniest smile to let him know it's not his fault, and Mortimer appreciates that.

"I'm so sorry, my..."

"Don't. It's fine, Dave. I get it. It's business. It's business. It's business. It's business. It's business. It's business. It's business. It's business," Caroline becoming more irate every time she says, 'It's business.' Caroline picks up the phone and starts dialling some random (555) number.

"Who are you angrily calling?" asks Dave, using inquiring thoughts.

"Brenda!" snaps Caroline. "At least she wants to spend time with me! And you know what's sad and also gross, but mostly gross?! Unlike you, I know she won't waste time to see what I look like below my navel!"

Both Caroline and Dave instantly wretch profusely at the thought of Brenda doing sexy things. Regaining her gag reflex's composure, she tells Dave to leave. Dave wretches again, this time getting a little on his business coat. It's grey – the coat, not the the puke.

"Can we talk about this?" pleads Dave.

Mortimer presses his fins together and prays in solidarity alongside him.

"Hi Brenda, come over. I need consoling. I'm dealing with angry feelings," sobs Caroline. "Yes, it's about Dave." The phone clicks and suddenly there's a knock at the door.

"IT'S ME! BRENDA! YOUR BEST FRIEND!"

"Well, that's brutally pathetic," scoffs Dave.

Dave has lived his entire existence without many regrets, but introducing Caroline to Brenda at the community's barn dance social three years ago is by far his biggest. To be fair, it wasn't his fault. Brenda was wearing an ascot that day and Dave mistook it for a contest ribbon. He mistakenly thought she was a prized pig. Dave only wanted to show Caroline because she adores snouted animals. Since that day Brenda has infiltrated their lives, relentlessly spending every waking moment trying to end their relationship. She wants Caroline for herself, and Dave knows if she can she will kill him in a second to make that murder happen. What makes the situation worse is that Brenda also happens to live across the hall from Caroline, so technically, Dave can be assassinated at any given moment. Fuck, that has to be stressful for poor Dave.

"KNOCK! KNOCK! KNOCK!" Brenda snorts, banging on Caroline's door again with her muddy hoof. Probably.

Reluctantly Dave opens the door.

"David," Brenda oinks.

"Brendan," Dave enunciates with perfect English.

Brenda shoves Dave hard to the side as she waddles towards Caroline, wearing an Oreo moo-moo she made out of thirty-nine bathroom towels, acting like her irrelevant feelings aren't hurt, but deep down she knows he got to her. She prepackages her emotions so she can eat them later.

Dave stares at Caroline longingly, pining, making sure she can see in his eyes that he's sorry and loves her unconditionally. "I'll call you after I get all my business done. Please forgive me."

Caroline leans her head against Brenda's beef shoulder.

Walking out feeling as if he's entering his villain origin story, Dave closes the door. "I have to be an upgraded man," he says determinedly. "I will defeat Brenda and business once and for all. Caroline and I will have our happily ever after." Dave takes the elevator down this time and begrudgingly goes to do business.

Back at Caroline's place, Mortimer is emotionally wrecked, blowing stress bubbles like crazy, trying to grasp what the fuck happened. Mortimer has to do something. But what? He's only a goldfish. Then as if one of those Biblical miracles that magically appear which we always hear about but have zero scientific proof to back the claims, Mortimer gets an idea. He knows exactly what to do — how to save the greatest love story of our generation and more importantly... make Dave his new dad.

BUSINESS AND BRENDA ARE VILLAINS

While Dave heads to the office where so much business is waiting for him, Business is plotting evil intentions as villains do. What Dave didn't realize is that his undying passion for business had manifested into a physical being, one who became insanely hellbent on destroying Dave and Caroline's relationship. Sitting on a gilded inkwell, practicing its most diabolical laughter, Business is ready for its big reveal. Business has become a live-action supply closet. With ominously sharpened 2H pencils for a woody body and limbs, woven together with unfurled and spiralled paperclips, two silver thumb-tacked eyes, a hole punch reinforcement mouth, and a black quill stuck into its eraser for hair, Business is primed to be the only true love in Dave's life.

Rolling up to his building of business Enter Prizes, parking in his reserved spot, Dave can spider sense something is wrong. This sickening feeling comes over him. Whether it's the thought of losing Caroline forever or realizing he forgot to close his office blinds, he can't quite figure out the mystery. Dave walks into his establishment of business and heads up to the 3rd floor. That's where he does all his business. Reading the Polka Dot Door with the name Dave on it, he verifies that he indeed has found his office.

"Ah, I love business so much." Dave takes a deep breath to relish in his accomplishments.

Turning the doorknob, entering his body inside his office, Dave can't wait to get lots of business done, but as he reaches for the Care Bear-themed light switch, his Elmo desk lamp turns on.

As the light illuminates Business' presence, Business does a Dr. Claw impression with a Hello Kitty eraser, "Good eeeevening, Dave. Have a seat."

"Who are you?" Dave asks in a confused manner, taking a seat in his Alf replica office chair.

"I'm Business," says Business. "Let's talk." Business jumps

down from the inkwell and begins pacing back and forth on Dave's no-assembly-required desk like a stationery dictator. "Dave listen, you're getting far behind on business. I need you to put in more hours at the office. I understand Caroline is very important to you but try and see it from my point of view. It's business. Without you, business will never become the global business that you've been striving for this business to be."

"Go on," Dave being all inspired and shit, forgetting how mad he is that Business manifested itself using his office supplies without asking.

"If you want business to succeed, I'm going to need you to stay in the office to perform business for three months. You can't leave, not even to see Caroline," demands Business.

"Can she at least come and see me?" Dave asks.

"No. You can't have any distractions. If she really loves you, she'll still be there waiting for you even if you cut all ties and communication with her," Business coerces slyly.

"That will be a true test of our love," says Dave. "Alright, I'm convinced. Let's make this business the best business a business can be!" Dave starts working on business right away.

"MUAHAHAHAHAHA!" Business laughing sinisterly as office supplies can.

Dave smiles. "Gosh, you're cute," poking its belly with his index finger.

"Don't touch me!" Business scolding Dave with a slap on his finger with one of its pencil lead hands. "Now give me your phone. I don't trust you. I promise after three months when I'm a global empire, I'll let you see Caroline again."

Dave always dreamed of business reaching every corner of the globe, and as much as he'll miss Caroline because romance is like that, he knows if he can put a stranglehold on every other business in the world, he and Caroline can live the perfect life he always dreamed of.

Dave reluctantly gives Business his recycled Captain Planet-inspired phone. "Okay, three months and then you let me go back to Caroline so I can see what she looks like below her navel. Do we have ourselves a deal?"

Business takes Dave's cool phone and just throws it in the garbage can. With a diabolical smile, it stretches out one of his pencil arms and shakes Dave's hand. "You have got yourself a deal. Now let's do some me!"

Dave gets to work right away. As he types furiously on his Osborne I laptop's keyboard, Business does a pirouette, because it knows that Dave doesn't know he'll never see Caroline again. Damn, Business is toxic as fuck.

Back at Caroline's condo, Caroline is crying. She and Dave have never fought like that before. She notices she's starting to receive some bad feelings from her heart. She has to make it right. Wasting no time, she picks up her moderately priced phone to call Dave.

Brenda knocks the phone out of her hands with her hoof. "What are you doing?!"

"I need to call Dave. I want to apologize for how I acted. He needs to know I still love him and that there's no one else I want to show what I look like below my navel to," Caroline crying the most believable tears.

"I got a better idea. How about you don't so I can express all my deepest feelings for you? Wouldn't your brain like to accept those kinds of desperate pleas or better yet, your heart? I have a plethora of consonants and vowels I'd like to string together into a lengthy and emotionally unstable confession if you allow me," begs Brenda like a small dog wanting up because a bigger dog is coming towards her.

Caroline looks deep into Brenda's yellow eyes caused by jaundice and gives her a wistfully wistful smile, remembering how Brenda contracted hepatitis by that mall Santa with the trucker's hat she met behind Walmart two years ago. Brenda has an affinity for meeting bad men, but Caroline knows sometimes romance is like that.

"Yes Brenda, express yourself at me. The floor is yours," offers Caroline.

Brenda immediately honks some irritable 'I'll die without you' sob story about how she lost the urge for unprotected sex by shady men to falling in love with Caroline and wanting nothing more than for her to permanently ditch Dave, so they can get married and show Caroline what true love looks like; she would prove that, unlike Dave, she wants to see what Caroline looks like below her navel and how it will be her life's mission to always make sure Caroline stays moist down there. Brenda licks her lips with her cigarette-stained tongue, the brown fuzz protruding from it, proving to Caroline she meant business, frisky business.

Caroline does her best to keep her stomach contents in place not wanting to be rude because Brenda is practically a friend of hers. She keeps it down, but the whole time she can't stop wondering why Brenda's left hand is missing. The curiosity is getting to her. She has to ask. "Brenda, what happened to your hoof? Did you accidentally devour it at that all-you-can-eat Chinese buffet place down the street? I told you you should wear oven mitts when you're eating. Sometimes you're the hungriest of hippos and don't pay attention to what you're doing."

Brenda slightly offended that Caroline would interrupt her Shakespearian spewing of undying love, yet remembering she has to play it cool because she knows this is her one shot to scissor her best friend into oblivion. She takes a deep breath and calmly obliges the answer Caroline asked for. Brenda began telling her how she was walking by the dog park earlier when she saw a chihuahua, so she put her hoof through the chain-link fence to pet it and the chihuahua bit her.

"It was quite the nuisance," Brenda exclaims. "I tried to pull my hoof out, but it got stuck. Next thing I knew five more chihuahuas were gnawing on it like it was an overstuffed burrito. It even made me hungry. I screamed for help, but everyone ignored me. As blood bled like an overanxious exterior designer painting the snow and bit by bit my hoof became more and more bite-size, I realized no one was going to help me."

"Yeah, I see that. Why do you think that is?" Caroline asks.

"Unfortunately, I made the mistake of trying to scissor four of their wives kind of like what I'm attempting with you."

Caroline throws up in her mouth a bit. "I see," Caroline subtly swallowing it back down. "Continue."

"And the fifth guy was the one who gave me herpes." And now you know where she got the herpes from. "He accused me that I was the one who gave it to him, not the other way around which is preposterous. When vaginas get acne it's the pussiest and I told him that. I swear male virgins don't know anything. Am I right?" Brenda definitely gave that guy herpes.

Caroline nods affirmatively, her face turning green.

"Men can be cruel, so misinformed sometimes. Thankfully the chihuahuas, super cute by the way, thankfully they ate enough of my hoof so I could get it free from the fence."

"Those poor, poor, poor chihuahas," empathetically states Caroline. Caroline hands Brenda a clean tissue to put on her bloody stump. Yes, Brenda has been bleeding all over the place this whole time.

It's at this moment Brenda knows she has to go in for the kill and finish expressing her unwavering love for Caroline. "Can I finish expressing my pure feelings in the same proximity as your ears, Caroline?" Brenda bellows.

"Fine. On one condition. Let me cauterize your stump and then you can clean up all this blood. I don't want Dave to show up thinking I let you in while you're on your period again." Caroline remembering the time Dave slipped, broke his glasses and ruined his new business suit he bought from Temu.

"You got yourself a deal!" salivates Brenda.

Taking out a small lighter from her pocket, which Caroline uses to delicately light her fragrantly scented candles, she starts scorch-earthing Brenda's bloody stump. The crackling sound of Brenda's flesh sizzling makes Caroline queasy, but it has to be done. Brenda doesn't make a sound. The smell of cooked ham puts her in a trance – barely fighting off the insatiable urge to dine and dash on herself. I fucking hate Brenda so much.

"There. Roasted to perfection." Caroline then hands her a Vileda broom. "I'm going to bed. Wake me up when Mr. Clean arrives and starts giving you a slow clap for a job well done."

Brenda grabs the broom; the feeling of the handle instantly makes her vagina secrete her mating slime. "I'm going to be on it," she says with a wink in her most seductive voice, similar to a hyena being rotisseried alive on an open fire.

Caroline heads upstairs to her bedroom, utilizing both of her feet as she climbs each step. One-footed Brenda watches on with jealousy as Caroline gracefully disappears from view. Brenda starts sweeping up the blood.

Mortimer, poor Mortimer is horrified by everything he's seen and heard because he couldn't bury himself underneath his rainbow-coloured pebbles far enough. He can't let this happen. He has to notify Dave quickly, somehow. He has to warn him before it's too late. Despite now being traumatized for the rest of his life, he has to put his fishy thinking cap on. He needs a solution. Come Hell or high water, Dave is going to be his new dad.

Not to be outdone by Mortimer's determination for life goals, as soon as Brenda went over to Caroline's to say revolting things to her, hoping Caroline would swoon on the idea of letting her see what she looks like below her navel, Cheddar wasted no time changing the lock of Brenda's condo.

"THANK. FUCK." Cheddar breathing a sigh of relief he's been waiting three years for, dragging his front paws down his face, shedding every iota of her existence from his mind. "Now I can finally get rid of that mouldy flour smell." Cheddar grabs a linen-scented Febreze spray bottle and gets right to work.

"Spritz, spritz, spritz spritz," spritzs the never used linen-scented Febreze spray bottle.

Cheddar's life is freshly amazing. He might just start a book club or an OnlyFans. The world is now his oyster. Cheddar is happy.

Ten hours later, Caroline wakes up with a big smile on her face, dripping profusely from a vivid sex dream she was enjoying. Dave was in the dream. Well, I'd imagine so. It would coincide with the amount of love she has for him and how well it fits in with the story. In her Golden Girls nightie, she heads downstairs to check on Brenda's progress. This should be good.

"Did you manage to clean up the blood, Brenda?" Caroline inspecting her place as she walks towards the foul scent of mouldy flour.

"Yes, every drop. You'll need a new broom though; the bristles didn't survive. Please don't be mad. I know how much you love this wide-angle broom and red Vileda Oskar's aren't cheap." Brenda sounding more pathetic and irritating than usual.

"It's alright. Just throw it in the garbage. I'll buy a new one tomorrow," Caroline reassuring Brenda confidently in a way that tells her she has a steady income.

Brenda twists off the brush end of the broom, her blood coagulated and caked between every bristle like an entire pack of red licorice with shedded candied skin, revealing they were black this whole time. Wow. That's so fucking deep. "I'm going to keep the broom handle though. Is that okay?" Brenda's body pulsates, quivers like a morning dew worm cut in half, imagining how much sexy pleasure she's going to give her pelvic cubby hole later tonight.

Caroline prays that Brenda merely has an overenthusiastic interest in hanging coats, that's why she's gyrating with excitement because she's planning to use it as a closet rod and not to flagpole herself. Her fingers have never been so crossed.

"Caroline?" Brenda continues being the needy attention-seeking wildebeest that she is. "Can I please finish expressing my deep feelings for you?" Brenda farts nervously, convincing herself

Caroline is enamoured with the flatulent display of flattery.

"Sure." Caroline swallowing another mouthful of vomit.

Brenda opens up her gaping horse mouth, drool pouring out between the gaps of her giraffe teeth, "Caroline, I love you."

Nope. Can't. Let's go check in on Dave again via time warp.

"Look at these numbers!" shouts Business.

Dave looks up at Business' PowerPoint presentation, he smiles successfully. He loves all the colours Business added to the graphs and pie charts. Dave puts his head back down and continues typing away feverishly on his Osborne 1 laptop. Dave's business is doing amazing business. He's never been happier, yet the thought of Caroline heavies his heart. A flash image of Brenda instantly gives him a migraine. "Tylenol!" Dave holding up his hand.

Business does a perfect Steph Curry fadeaway impression with the bottle and swishes it into Dave's palm. "Three points! Count it, bitch!" Business just absolutely jacked the fuck up about the room's synergy.

Dave pops the lid with one hand and swallows a mouthful, not making a single erroneous keystroke in the process. Man, Dave is so smooth. However, as high as Dave's business is hitting those margins and expanding his business at a cheetah's pace, he doesn't realize how fast his life is going by and the longer Business encourages Dave to be the imperial business tycoon he can be, every day more and more Dave thought less about Caroline and the dream they share: that one day she will show him what she looks like below her navel.

Picture this: You know those funny day and night scenes in cartoons where the sun and moon go up and down, up and down at ungodly speeds? Well, that's what's happening in real-time. Dave doesn't know it but what feels like three hours is actually three years. Yes, comically Dave has been doing nonstop business for three years. That's why whenever you look at a business you think about Dave. Enter Prizes has been dominating the economic world, and even recently Forbes Magazine unanimously voted him as the

World's Sexiest & Most Efficient Businessman In Business. Dave's business became everything he hoped it to be. Yet there's a voice nagging at him, that something is wrong, but he can't finger it out.

Dave leans back on his Alf replica chair, "Business, do you mind if I take a break? It's been three hours."

"I guess," Business retorts begrudgingly because Business is a fucking Bic head.

"Can you also bring me today's newspaper as awkwardly as possible? I want to see if there's been any new news in the last three hours."

Business obliges, after all, what possibly can go wrong? It has Dave exactly where it wants him. Business does a handspring off the projector projecting its PowerPoint presentation to Dave and tippy tips its way down the stairs to fetch the newspaper.

As Business fetches the newspaper haphazardly for Dave, Dave ponders what can be bothering him. He is thinking adult thoughts. "What can it be?" Dave wonders to himself.

All of a sudden, Business huffs into the office completely out of breath with the newspaper, cursing and swearing. Well, that was fast. "You have too many damn stairs! You need to get that fucking elevator fixed! Do you have any idea how many times I had to go up and down those stairs, to get this newspaper up here?!"

"The elevator does work. The 'OUT OF ORDER' sign is so that no one else uses it. It's mine. Besides, maybe if you didn't make me fire everyone, I could have gotten someone else to get the newspaper for me, you know, someone with poseable thumbs."

Business dagger-stares Dave right in the eyes and mouths, "FUCK. YOU."

Dave grabs the newspaper off the floor and as if he saw a spooky ghost his jaw drops, signifying something relevant to the story has happened. On the front page is a picture of Caroline and Brenda kissing – the ultra-bold headline reads: "SCUBA DIVING EQUIPMENT HEIRESS TO MARRY WHATEVER THAT IS BESIDE HER NEXT WEEK!" Dated three years into the future. Really? I had no freaking idea Caroline is an heiress to a huge fortune. Good for her not allowing that to cloud her dreams of working for a marketing firm that specializes in children dying from cancer. This story is just writing itself now.

Dave drops the newspaper, his Osborne 1 laptop's screen revealing his reflection somewhat clearly but not really because its screen is only five inches wide. "OH MY GOD! WHAT IS GOING ON?!" Dave runs his fingers through his long black hair and bushy beard. "What is happening? What did you do?" screams Dave, struggling with some pretty dreadful feelings.

Business stands upright, pointing sternly at Dave. "I made you a success story. I made you super rich. I made you relevant," speaks Business in its best rendition of a calculative James Bond villain voice.

"NOOOOOOOO WAAAAAAAAAAAY!" Dave's lungs reverberating from his extended use of vowels. "I have to stop that wedding. Fuck! Fax Machine! My parrot! I also have to stop him from being malnourished and dehydrated! I hope it's not too late!" Dave turns to Business, picks it up and as brutally as anyone can in vengeance mode, hits Business with the coldest line ever written in the literary world, "Business is closed." Dave throws Business into his Samurai Pizza Cat pencil case.

Business pleads. "Wait! Stop! Can't you see I did this for you?! I love y…"

Dave doesn't give any shits. He zips the pencil case shut and tosses it into his Oscar The Grouch garbage can. Pleading is what happens when you run out of bargaining chips for those who are unfamiliar with guilt.

Dave makes a determination fist. "I got to make this right. It's not too late." Dave timely pauses, waiting for the audience to applaud. The silence tells him that he's not in a movie but in a book. He slowly puts his fist down as he sweats from embarrassing feelings. "I'm getting my girl back. Caroline I'm coming to see what you look like below your navel!" Dave rushes out the door and towards his electric bike.

    Alas, an unfortunate plot twist happens. Someone stole his electric bike, but nothing is going to stop Dave from getting there as quickly as possible. Dave walks home, making sure only to step in previously walked footprints in the snow. He has plans to draw up. The most epic love story the world has ever seen is going to get the proper ending it deserves. Dave begins tiptoeing through the crunchy crisp snow like a whimsical flamingo performing a mesmerizing dance number. At this pace, he'll be home in no time. He just hopes it isn't too late to get Caroline back, and that somehow Fax Machine survived 1095 days of neglectful parenting. Dave is ready to be the man he should have always been.

LOVE IS NOT A TRIFORCE

Dave stands at the door of his apartment, his hand on the doorknob, preparing for the worst. Reminiscing on all the fond memories he and Fax Machine had, he opens the door and walks inside, and there is Fax Machine's skeleton – super dead. Dave falls to his knees and man cries, tears falling so manly some would say they weren't even there at all. Scoping around his apartment he sees gnaw marks in the drywall. Yes, Fax Machine was eating drywall for nourishment. He did asbestos he could to survive. As you can see, it didn't work. Dave's heart sinks with major guilty feelings. Fax Machine didn't deserve to go out like that. Dave is a very naughty parrot dad. Dave slaps his hand as hard as he can. He deserves to be punished. As his hand turns slightly red from the hefty smack, he knows exactly what he has to do.

Gently he picks up Fax Machine, caresses his skeleton and walks towards the window. He opens it, gives Fax Machine the biggest hug and whispers, "How about one last flight, little buddy?" Dave then holds Fax Machine in his hand like a football and throws the most beautiful spiral. Dave dries his eyes knowing Fax Machine would be proud of how far he was able to throw him. Dave can rest easy knowing God caught him for the perfect touchdown. "Goodbye, my friend. We'll meet again someday. I love you." Dave closes the window and starts his grandiose plan to get Caroline back.

Pulling out multi-coloured construction paper, Crayons, markers, tape, scissors, glue, rulers, thumbtacks, highlighters, and his Teenage Mutant Ninja Turtles stapler complete with staples, Dave is ready to put a complex plan in place that will make Kevin McCallister proud. Dave didn't pull out an eraser, because Dave is amazing at arts and crafts. He won't need it. Go ahead. Ask his parents. They will confirm it. They still have his macaroni art from kindergarten up on their fridge. Dave's parents are always proud of his creations. Not like my parents, but this story isn't about me. It's an epic love story about the love shared between two fictional characters. Dave gets working on his spectacular plan on how to stop Caroline from committing certain acts of bestiality with Brenda. He just hopes he's not too late.

"I need to stop Caroline from committing certain acts of bestiality with Brenda. I just hope I'm not too late," Dave says, confirming what I said he was thinking.

Twenty minutes go by, and Dave creates the greatest plan. You should see it. He's incorporated so many details, colours, and the use of scented markers really brings the whole thing to life. I know you can't see it, but without question, it's worth five out of five stars.

"I'm getting my girl back. Her name is Caroline. This plan is foolproof. Afterwards, I'm giving it to my parents so they can expand my legacy on their refrigerator." Dave fist bumps himself knowing what he just said is one hundred percent correct. "I've got this," Dave says, completing the boost of his confidence. He rolls up his master plan and makes his way to Caroline's condo.

The first thing you see in this scene are two majestic brown Clydesdale horses trotting up to Caroline's condo building. Dave wants to make a grand entrance, because this is his moment, and it needs to be exquisite if he has any chance of getting Caroline back. To Dave's surprise, Caroline isn't conveniently waiting for him at the front of her building.

"I probably should've grabbed my phone when I left the office so I could have given her a heads up," Dave tells himself insightfully. So far, his plan is not planning out well as most good plans usually plan out. Dave undeterred about the small hiccup, gets off the carriage and pays the reigns master with a 58% tip. Dave is always generous. That's why everyone loves Dave. Well, except Brenda, but to be fair gelatinous balls of slime can't be accountable for how they feel. Dave is not bothered that she has the cellular structure of a wet balloon. Besides, he loves Caroline.

Her opinion of him and her unrequited love is all he needs.

Dave doesn't buzz Caroline's condo number. He has a key. Just one of the perks of dating someone for thirty-three years. Technically thirty-six. Fucking try it sometime. Letting himself in like he's been living there for a while, Dave takes the elevator. Dave wanted to take the stairs since it's been three years since he's done any sort of real exercise, but that's not what he drew up on his super cool plan. He has to stick to it or risk losing his beloved forever. Man, I wish you can see the exquisite plan Dave made. It's impressive even for Dave. Just picture an absolute banger of a plan created by ethereal beings from outer space and times that by a million. That's one percent of how amazing it is. Ding. Dave reaches Caroline's floor. It's been a hot minute since I mentioned what floor it's on... Is it the 8th floor? Do you even care about that tidbit of information? No. Fuck your selfish need for precise storytelling.

Dave walks out of the elevator when its doors open as per proper elevator protocol states and steps onto the 13th floor. Walking down the hallway, excitement sticking to Dave's entire body like multi-coloured foam being sprayed on a BMW going through a carwash, he makes his way to Caroline's condo which is situated on the 24th floor. And like that, Dave stands at Caroline's door.

Dave checks his plan. "Yup, suite number eight on the 10th floor." Dave reassures to himself that his plan is fucking fantastic. This is it. This is the moment Dave worked so hard for, waited for. At suite number eight, Caroline's condo on the 35th floor, he knocks three times on her door. The three knocks are important to his plan. They signify that Dave's dominance over Caroline's heart is about to be established. Brenda doesn't stand a goat-milking chance in fucking Hell to even retain two percent of Caroline's love. Dave knows he has this in the bag. Dave is so suave. Dave does a subtle hair flip, doubling down on how cool he looks right now.

The door opens and Dave's skin colour runs away in fright. For clarification Dave is Caucasian.

"What are you doing here?!" Brenda scolds, topless, wearing nothing but one of Caroline's red curtains as a towel.

Dave stutters. "Uh… uh… uh…" Holding up his dubious plan to Brenda's face, Dave explains to Brenda what he's doing here. Suddenly her cosmic mass begins sucking Dave in with its gravitational pull; he grabs the door jamb, doing his best not to get swallowed. "This is not a part of my plan," informs Dave.

"Give me that!" Brenda howls loudly, taking Dave's perfect plan out of his hand.

"Hey, give that back! It's mine! I need it to ruin your life so I can better mine!" he cries.

"Oh really? What happens when I do this?" Brenda then fatly shoves Dave's outstanding plan into her mouth and eats it, because that's how Brenda deals with all of her problems.

"NOOOOOOOOOOO WAAAAAAAAAAAY!" Dave screams. "It can't be true! You have thwarted my attempt to win Caroline's love back!" Dave falls to his knees in defeat but quickly stands up when he gets a glimpse of what's under Brenda's curtain. So many tentacles. Dave throws up on Brenda, and Brenda smirks knowing without Dave's tubular plan, he will never see what Caroline looks like below her navel.

"What's with the cacophonous ruckus?" Caroline walking behind Brenda, not looking too impressed that Brenda wrecked another one of her fucking curtains.

Brenda's backfat tracks backwards like a Mephisthophelean horse struggling with obesity and neighs a final insult, as she lets Caroline have her turn talking to Dave.

"Yes? What do you want, Dave?" asks a perturbed Caroline, wearing a proper towel, staying cool as a cucumber because she damn well knows Brenda doesn't eat vegetables.

"You can't marry Brenda. I love you!" Dave confessing his love without the use of animal sounds.

Caroline takes a deep breath before speaking because she knows her reply is going to be long-winded, "Why? I thought you died without me and without the courtesy of telling me. You broke my heart. I know Brenda is an organism no one in the right mind would want, but you were gone for so long. I was lonely, and honestly, whenever I needed to show someone what I look like below my navel, Brenda was there."

Caroline and Dave puke in unison.

"I'll get the broom." Brenda disfiguredly gallops to the utility closet where Caroline keeps a cache of brooms now for special occasions like the one she's having with Dave.

Dave caresses a few stray chunks of what looks to be pita bread from her mouth with his business coat's sleeve. Caroline doesn't repay the favour, because she's still very mad at him. Dave forgives her and wipes his own mouth with no judgment because romance is like that. He then goes on to tell Caroline everything that happened in the last three years. Caroline instantly forgives him and passionately kisses Dave on the mouth with her mouth. Dave accepts it. That happened because Caroline is super kind, understanding and never stopped loving Dave. She knows they're soulmates. Also, I didn't want to write all the potential dialogue between the two of them just for the sake of something as asinine as continuity. Way too much fucking work for this indie author. Fight me.

Brenda sees what true love is supposed to resemble as she angrily grips the broom. She really, really hates Dave. "No! I don't care! You're too late, Dave! Caroline and I are getting married and there's nothing you can do about it!" Brenda pulls Caroline away from Dave like she's choosing her favourite breadstick from the wicker basket of a fancy restaurant. "She's mine!"

Caroline rips her arm from Brenda's hoofy grip. "Don't ever touch me again! We are done! Dave is the love of my life and you're nothing! Not even worthy of being some nonsensical, disgusting character in some shit author's satirical romance novella! Get.

Out!"

Brenda panics and blames Cheddar. "It's not my fault. If Cheddar never locked me out of my condo, we never would have become roommates and this whole situation would have been avoided." Brenda is a fucking liar. We know she wanted Caroline since day one. Let's see what else she blabs on about. Brenda pathetically goes on to say, "Okay. Okay. How about this? How about the three of us get married and we can be one big happy family? Come on, guys, my vagina is versatile. This could work. Please for old times' sake? Let's start over. I'll even go first. Dave, I love you, and I want nothing more than for you as well to see what I look like below my navel because romance is like that."

Dave and Caroline try their best not to purge and upchuck their feelings. They succeed and kiss to celebrate.

"Brenda, you've wasted three years of my life. I don't want to ever see you again. Now get out!" Caroline pointing across the hall of the 92nd floor to where Brenda used to live.

At the same time, Cheddar is walking to his door with a bag of groceries. Caroline acknowledges Cheddar's feline existence, "Hi Cheddar, how are you?"

Cheddar gives Caroline a quick nod and dashes for the door as Brenda makes a beeline for it too. By a fraction, Cheddar is able to get in and lock the door behind him. Brenda turns towards Caroline and Dave, but they've already closed and locked the door behind them as well.

"I will have my revenge," Brenda threatens, as the boils on her scales begin to pus litres of guacamole. On the bright side, at least Brenda doesn't have to walk far to get out of the building since she's on the 1st floor.

Caroline pulls Dave into the living room by his business coat's collar, kissing him with her lips. "I fucking missed you, you handsome man."

Before Dave can repeat something in the same manner, he's interrupted by emphatic blubs blubbing. It's Mortimer just losing his absolute ever fucking mind.

"BLUB! BLUB!" Mortimer swimming laps around his bowl like a racecar, jumping out of his bowl and doing an array of flips that could easily get him past Cirque De Soleil auditions. His dad is back. Mortimer has his dad back.

Dave sees Mortimer, kisses Caroline and says, "One second, beautiful." Dave walks up to Mortimer and gives his head a little head pat with his index finger. "I missed you too, pal."

Mortimer just fucking dies. No, literally. The excitement got to Mortimer so much that his heart exploded. Kidding. I think one animal's death is enough for this love story. To be honest, I'm having regrets killing off Fax Machine. If it makes you feel better it wasn't really part of the plan, but I'm writing this novella so fast, that I'm not putting enough thought into the storytelling and not thinking straight, so if Fax Machine's death traumatized you, I'm sorry. It wasn't intentional. As it stands Mortimer is very much alive and is the happiest goldfish in the whole universe.

Dave turns around and goes back to Caroline. They kiss. It's then Caroline looks at Dave like she needs nothing more than to be train-yarded. Sorry. Railed. Caroline looks like she needs to be railed. The expression of Dave's beaming grin on his face tells her he's ready to be a conductor.

Grabbing her towel around her waist, she seductively states her current mindset and says, "Do you want to see what I look like below my navel?"

Without hesitation, Dave says, "Yes."

As Caroline goes to pull off her towel, a sickening feeling comes over Dave like a tsunami of fluid water. "Wait. Hold on," he says. "Something is wrong."

"What's wrong?" whimpers Caroline.

"I don't know but I'm sensing something terribly evil is going to happen."

"What could it be? We're together. Brenda is gone, and look at Mortimer, he's so happy."

"Blub, blub, blub," Mortimer dancing a smooth waltz with his decorative deep sea diver.

"Caroline, I can't explain it but I feel like there's a terrible evil about to be unleashed," Dave warns; his penis hardened, because despite the ominous feeling, a part of him wants nothing more than to locomotive Caroline's tunnel bridge. "I think we're in grave danger. I think we need to prepare for Mortal Kombat."

"You're scaring me? What do you mean?" sweet Caroline tightening her towel around her waist, knowing that today won't be the day Dave sees what she looks like below her navel.

"I'm not sure but I sense we're going to find out soon." Dave stares off into the distance to properly segue into the next scene of this perfectly written chapter.

And Dave isn't kidding. He isn't wrong. Something indeed is afoot. Allow me to justify Dave's worries which are prime examples of foreshadowing. What Dave didn't realize when he was explaining everything to her of what happened over the last three years was that Brenda had pressed her runny elephant's trunk up against the door and eavesdropped on Dave and Caroline's private conversation. There was probably supposed to be a comma in there somewhere. That is why Brenda is standing lopsided in Dave's business office, searching for... that's right... BUSINESS! Sorry for the shouting; it was for dramatic effect. Don't worry, I am aware the timing of all this isn't quite adding up. I also don't give a fuck. So there's that.

Brenda finds Dave's Samurai Pizza Cats pencil case and carefully opens it up. Inside it, Business is shaking, murmuring to itself.

"Hello Business," Brenda grunts.

Business turns and sees Brenda and pukes up some pencil shavings. "Who the hell are you and why are your scales covered in guacamole?" questions Business.

"First of all, they're not scales, they're shingles and my name is Brenda not Who. Listen. I have a proposition for you," Brenda claims with her spot-on Cyril Sneer impression.

"What... What is it?" Business curious but also fearful of this monstrous creature staring at it like maybe she just might stuff herself with it.

"Vengeance. I want us to team up to get our revenge on Dave and Caroline. Dave broke your heart. Caroline broke mine. The only natural response is to murder them in cold blood. Are you with me?"

Business is so excited about the dubious idea that it forgets how grotesque Brenda is. "Yes, let's team up and kill some people we know," crawling out of the Samurai Pizza Cats pencil case with the utmost enthusiasm. Business climbs onto Brenda's hoof. "Let us scheme, lovely." Business doesn't realize it but Brenda's primal viciousness is tearing down its emotional guard. Business is about to be in for a shock because whether it believes it or not, it's well on its way to falling in love with Brenda. Why? Because terrible people deserve each other. Well, Brenda and Business aren't people per se, but you know what I mean.

EVERYTHING BAGEL WITH HERBS AND GARLIC CREAM CHEESE

"Wake up, my love. The sun is in the sky now," Caroline giving Dave a hefty hand push against his shoulder.

Despite the fear that something awful is about to happen, Dave was able to get the mandatory hours one person needs for an excellent night's sleep. He needed it too. You can imagine how tired he must have been being up for three straight years doing business.

Dave opens his eyes and puts a cast iron frying pan on the nightstand. He wasn't taking any chances. No one gets the jump on Dave. He wanted to be prepared in case of intruders. Dave turns to Caroline, puts his hand on her face in a non-abusive way and says, "I forgot to tell you that Fax Machine died." Dave's eyes get wet.

Caroline lovingly dries them. That was nice of her. "How did he manage that?"

"The inability to open a fridge mostly," Dave trying to keep a brave face.

Caroline hugs Dave with her arms. Dave feels loved and safe because he knows that's how proper hugs are executed. Caroline's eyes widen. Her brain jolts with an epiphany. "Hey, let's go out for breakfast. We can eat so we don't get hungry."

Dave is craving an everything bagel with herbs and garlic cream cheese. He can't let this opportunity get past him. "What a great idea. I'll even pay for my half of the bill."

Caroline knew right then and there that Dave had changed, that she's the only thing he wants because Caroline used to pay for everything. She'd never admit it, but Dave was a cheapskate. If he couldn't write it off as a business expense, he wouldn't pay. The future was looking bright. Finally, I'm getting this epic love story back on track.

"Where do you want to go for breakfast?" asks Dave.

"There's a new amazing breakfast place that opened up in town three months ago. It's called Baked Moods. They have the best everything bagel with herbs and garlic cream cheese in the entire province. Even their coffee is hot. It's a pretty fancy place, but we're celebrating. Want to go?"

Dave jumps out of bed still wearing his business suit, coat and shoes, "Let's go! I love hot beverages!"

I really should get Dave to take a shower, or at least change his clothes. I'll add it later. Caroline doesn't seem to mind so I'm sure it's fine.

Caroline laughs, "You're young at heart. I am fond of that certain aspect of you." Caroline gets up like a normal fucking person, walks over to Dave and gives him the biggest kiss she's ever allocated to someone. Dave melts. "I'm just going to get into the shower quick and put on some clothes that I haven't been wearing for three straight years." Dave couldn't agree more and allows her to do what she just told him.

"I'll meet you downstairs. I'm going to chill with a certain fish named Mortimer." Dave brushes his teeth with his tongue.

"I have an extra toothbrush if you want to brush your teeth in real life," offers Caroline.

"Okay, my mouth does feel like the inside of a petri dish. Thank you." Dave takes the toothbrush and puts it in his coat pocket.

"Maybe you'll want to take a shower with me and see what I look like like below my navel as well," suggests Caroline.

"No, thank you. I don't participate in genital sightseeing on an empty stomach," politely waving her off. Caroline understood. Dave hasn't eaten anything in three years so she didn't press.

"Alright, I'll be down in thirty-three minutes and thirty-three seconds. See you downstairs." She kisses Dave again, hiding the fact his words gave her vagina severe depression.

Dave widens his mouth with a smile. Kissing her always gives him satisfactory feelings. Dave heads for the bedroom door and goes downstairs to greet Mortimer. Caroline goes to the bathroom and removes her floral nightie. She isn't wearing any underwear. Yes, she's hot and naked, about to get soapy and wet. Did it just get humid in here? Such a hot scene. I'm getting the tingles down there. Anyway, Dave hears the shower turn on as he reaches the bottom of the stairs. I know. Stairs in a condo? How absurd. Guess it's just one of the many perks of being an heiress to a large scuba diving equipment fortune.

"If only my stomach was full, I could be up there getting the grand tour of what Caroline looks like below her navel, but romance is like that." Dave is sad, but optimistic because he knows Caroline's vagina is only an everything bagel with herbs and garlic cream cheese away. Dave casually struts into the living room where Mortimer is already up, waiting for him.

"Blub! Blub!" Mortimer is beside himself. His real dad is home. It isn't a dream. Mortimer knows in his tiny aquatic heart that his master plan has worked. Mortimer stayed positive and never gave up. Because of that and his determination to bring his family back together, he was able to execute his plan perfectly.

While Dave continues strutting towards Mortimer like a popular high school kid, Mortimer blows bubbles like a sexually aroused clam.

"Hey there, handsome, any big plans today? I missed you. I see you've missed me too. Can I tell you a secret?" Dave leans over to Mortimer's bowl and whispers, "I'm not going anywhere. Love you, buddy."

Mortimer swoons from the impact of Dave's convincing words. "Blub! Blub!" Mortimer screams as he gives Dave a wink and finger fin.

Now Caroline isn't like other women, in the sense that she was able to shower, get dressed, do her hair and makeup by the time you finished reading this page. That's much faster than the time she said she'd be ready in. Most modernized women need a goddamn fortnight to apply toothpaste on their toothbrush. I'm not a woman so I don't know this to be exactly true. However, it does for whatever reason take them forever to look maybe three percent hotter than they did before. What I do know is, that if I were a woman and a man wanted to see what I looked like below my navel, I'd be frantically squirting the tube into my mouth so fast, it would shame a colossal squid having an ink orgasm and be brushing my teeth like a meth-addicted Bob Ross. JUST. GET. IT. DONE. Yes, that is exactly what a guy would say. You can fact-check my penis.

"I'm ready to go." Caroline seductively interrupts Dave and Mortimer's bro time, doing her best She's All That impression as she comes down the stairs. The dress she's wearing is long and red.

Dave, awestruck by her beauty, picks up his jaw. "You look attractive, Caroline." His eyes wider than my ex-girlfriend's legs when her cousin is in town.

Dave reaches for Caroline's hand as one of her feet reaches the last step. Left? Right? Who gives a shit? Dave delicately grabs Caroline's hand. Which one? Use your fucking imagination. Dave is a gentleman and makes sure Caroline doesn't fall and break her neck. At this point, Dave is overwhelmed with the thought that soon he's going to have an everything bagel with herbs and garlic cream cheese inside his mouth and flush it down with a hot coffee. Dave's life is fucking stellar right now. Mortimer agrees. Dave and Caroline throw on their coats and head out the door. Well, Dave was already wearing his coat but whatever. As they walk out into the hallway, they see a shotgun sticking out of the mail slot of Cheddar's door across from them.

Dave puts the erect double barrel into his mouth and uses it as a megaphone so he can amplify his words to their maximum potential, "Not taking any chances eh, Cheddar," jokes Dave.

"Meow," Cheddar meows.

"You're a smart cat. Have a great day."

Cheddar meows, "Meow."

Dave and Caroline head towards the elevator from the 72nd floor, cause yeah, fuck those steps.

Down in the underground parking lot, Dave and Caroline walk towards her red sedan. Yes, it's been fixed since last time I've mentioned it. As they walk towards the red sedan, they both can't help feeling like they're Batman about to drive the Batmobile and fight crime. They simultaneously have a good chuckle about it. They kiss and get in the car through separate doors because going through the same door would be unnecessarily awkward which makes for bad storytelling. Caroline is allowed to drive because Dave is progressive. They kiss again because romance is like that. Caroline starts the engine and uses the steering wheel to get them in the direction they need to go. Caroline follows all the rules of the road. The fewer red lights Caroline blows through, the more confident Dave feels letting Caroline be in control of an automated vehicle that has the ability to kill them both in a horrific accident. Vehicular manslaughter is one way to ruin a hot date. I'm looking at you unnamed celebrities. Look at that. Our lovers have arrived at their destination and no one died.

"You've earned this, love." Dave hands Caroline a smiley sticker to show how much he approves of her driving abilities.

Caroline blushes. "Thank you. I will cherish this forever." She places it inside a secret pocket in her leather flower purse where women typically misplace their shit. She zips it up, signifying that the smiley sticker gives her clout.

They get out of the car; the sound of snow crunching below their feet lets them know it's practically winter. High heels were a bad idea, Caroline. Walking to the front door of Baked Moods, they hold hands. They're happy. They're in love. They're getting breakfast.

Dave and Caroline breathe a sense of relief. There's no line. They can thank me later. I wasn't about to have them stand in line and be forced to write extra dialogue to fill a scene until it was their turn to order or feel obligated to write dialogue for other people standing in line that I don't even fucking know. No one has time for that shit.

Caroline orders an everything bagel with herbs and garlic cream cheese and a medium hot coffee. It's Dave's time to shine. He's been waiting for this moment for what feels like his entire life. Dave also orders an everything bagel with herbs and garlic cream cheese and shocks everyone behind the counter, pulling no punches and says, "Double toasted please."

"No one in history has ever requested that," explains the cashier. "We'll try our best to give your teeth the desired crunch you're expecting. So freaking cool, man!" continues the cashier that is clearly going fucking nowhere in life.

Dave looks down at the cashier's name tag. "Thank you, Timothy, and I will have a medium hot coffee as well," in his best David Caruso voice.

Dave hasn't realized it yet, but the whole time Caroline was ogling him hard like a high school girl with no self-respect. She wants Dave and she wants him now. Is it normal to be jealous of characters you've created? Sorry. I'm starting to believe if I were as cool as Dave, I could have kept my marriage from failing. Okay. I'm wrecking the story. Continuing on. Caroline pays for the food.

A short amount of time passes by. Fast food is like that. "Order #429!" Timothy calls out boldly as if he's a significant character in this story.

Dave looks at his receipt. Recognizing that the number matches the number Timothy said, he knows Timothy is referring to their order. Dave grabs the tray of food and drinks. Caroline watches Dave grab the tray of food and drinks. Sure, Dave didn't offer to pay for his meal like he said he would, but Dave still knows how to pull off sick, high-class chivalry stunts. Grabbing that tray of food and drinks is merely a sample of his gentlemanly prowess. Caroline's heart flutters. Dave may be cheap, but that's what makes him so successful at business. Caroline doesn't care. The fact that

Dave lifted and carried that tray of food and drinks all the way to their table without being asked was enough to convince Caroline they are meant to be. Dave puts the tray of food and drinks down without spilling a single drop of coffee. Lids are like that. The tray of food and drinks is dry. Not Caroline though, her vagina is wet. She can't control her fire hydrant feelings seeing Dave be courteous and smooth, corralling an everything bagel with herbs and garlic cream cheese, a medium hot coffee, an everything bagel with herbs and garlic cream cheese double toasted, a medium hot coffee and not making a mess. Caroline has a vulva and it's pulsating. Dave is happy he saved the eight dollars.

    Dave sits down on the chair and immediately unwraps his double toasted everything bagel with herbs and garlic cream cheese. He's excited. Caroline sits down on the chair. SQUELCH. Her panties moisturized by overproducing vaginal glands. She sips her coffee casually, pretending it's business as usual. Dave can't believe how delicious his double toasted everything bagel with herbs and garlic cream cheese is. He's on cloud nine. Caroline is on the verge of having an orgasm in public. Taking a bite of her everything bagel with herbs and garlic cream cheese, she can see why Dave's mouth is tickling his earlobes. She can tell Dave's taste buds are happy doing what they are designed for. What a perfect morning. They're happy. They're in love. They're eating breakfast.

    Dave swallows the last bite of his double toasted everything bagel with herbs and garlic cream cheese and looks out the window. "Whoa, the snow is on a downward trajectory."

    "You're right," agrees Caroline. "It's snowing."

    Suddenly they're shocked, for whom do you think they see appear outside in a blizzard I poorly described? That's right, it's that bitch Brenda. She walks right up to the window and smiles a wicked smile, her eyes rolling in the back of her head like The Undertaker after Tombstone Piledriving someone; her red beady eyes demonically reset and come back into frame, galvanized with disappointment because once again they failed to escape from her stupid face. She puts her carp lips against the window and mouths, "You're dead, Dave."

Dave doesn't react. He can't make out what she said because her mandibles are in the way.

"I think she's saying she's hungry," assumes Caroline.

Dave is not the least bit worried. He finished his double toasted everything bagel with herbs and garlic cream cheese which means she isn't able to steal it from him. Dave and Caroline begin to laugh because they know they are so in love, happy and full of breakfast, and Brenda has nothing – exactly what she deserves.

Brenda is hurt with enraged feelings; she donkey punches the window hard and nefariously pulls something out of her gooey kangaroo pouch.

Dave is horrified as he sees Brenda holding up a Samurai Pizza Cats pencil case. "No, it can't be!" Dave yells.

Caroline drops her hot coffee, shocked, because she knows exactly what the big reveal is going to be since Dave just recently told her everything. Staring at the surprising, not-so-surprising twist that's about to unfold, they glare as the pencil case zipper eventually unzips. It got stuck a couple of times on the fabric. As suspected it's Business and it's pissed off. It dead-stares Dave right in the eyes and with all the intensity of a 2H pencil, motions one of its lead hands across where its neck would be if it had one. Business is not fucking around. It has Dave's number and Dave knows it. Business then sinks methodically back down into the darkness of its Samurai Pizza Cats pencil case like an unplugged Whack-A-Mole game during midplay as Brenda slithers… Sorry. Sorry. Hold on. The zipper is stuck again. Give Business a second here… Okay… Okay… Yup… Nope… Not quite… Almost… Almost… THERE! GOT IT! As Brenda slithers back into what is an established super blizzard at this point, Business zips itself back up, laughing maniacally; Business is going to have vengeance. Brenda thinks the same thing, but no one gives a shit what Brenda thinks so who fucking cares. Both leave the scene at the same time.

"We need a plan," suggests Dave.

"You're right. This has got to stop," Caroline with her two cents.

"Are you thinking what I'm thinking, breakfast partner?" Dave clearly having a eureka moment.

Dave and Caroline affirmatively nod their heads in unison at each other and simultaneously shout, "MORTIMER!"

MORTIMER'S PLAN

Driving back to Caroline's condo, Dave sits in the passenger seat, allowing Caroline to drive again, because she successfully got them to Baked Moods without killing them in a fiery car wreck. Dave holds Caroline's hand lovingly, trusting she knows how to drive with one hand, and goes on to say, "Okay, we both agree that Mortimer has the best plans. After all, his last plan despite being risky and wild was able to bring us back together and get us on track, so one day I'll be able to see what you look like below your navel. He'll know how to get rid of Brenda and Business from our lives permanently."

Caroline nods with a high approval rating, yet nervously, because she's never driven with one hand before. She tries to keep her composure by white-knuckling the steering wheel. Refusing to let go of Dave's hand even though there's a chance she might not be able to make a slight turn and end up crashing into a row of pedestrians, she continues to risk the lives of innocent bystanders, because romance is like that. As Caroline safely makes it past the three-kilometre mark, her female confidence gradually grows as the temperature between her legs increases. Nonchalantly she moves Dave's hand closer to her vagina's temporal lobe — her clitoris throbbing as its personal bubble is about to burst. Closer, closer; every centimetre closer, her vagina needs less and less moisturizer. Dave would have never let his hand get so near before. In the past, Dave only cared about business, but Dave is different now. Thanks to Mortimer's plan, Caroline is his business now. Closer, closer... Caroline looks at Dave, biting her lip with anticipation, begging for Dave's unrequited participation.

Dave looks at Caroline, then his hand-holding hand, then back at Caroline, leans over to her and whispers in her ear in a manly passenger princess tone, "Keep your eyes on the road. I don't want to die."

Caroline knows Dave's suggestion is right — dying before hearing Mortimer's plan is not a correct decision. She lets go of Dave's hand and makes it so she has more than one hand on the steering wheel. "I'm sorry," Caroline whimpers.

"It's okay. You've never had me judge your driving before." Dave kisses Caroline on the cheek, showing he's forgiven her for putting her hormones before their own safety.

As Caroline pulls up to her condo building, she's sweating, unable to think straight. Her mind is swamped with too many sexy images of Dave taking a peek under her dress because that's where below her navel is. She can't think clearly and forgets what floor she lives on. "Dave, sweetie, I'm having pleasant thoughts and can't remember what floor I live on, can you remind me please?"

"The fifth."

Caroline is thankful Dave knew because there's a chance they could have gotten lost in there and died. Probably because I keep changing what floor she lives on. "I'm thankful," replies Caroline.

Dave knows she's thankful, but he has to ask, "Wait. Did you drive this whole way without your seatbelt on?"

Caroline is ashamed. She's lucky her vagina didn't cause her body to have the flexibility of a crash test dummy. She could have died. Caroline loves Dave.

"I did. I forgot. Sorry, love." Caroline isn't lying.

Lovers don't lie to each other. Caroline gets out of her red sedan, and walks to Dave's door, opening it to let him out. She owed him that much. Dave gets out feeling slightly perturbed by Caroline's poor decision-making but forgives her because romance is like that. The red sedan is completely void of people. Dave and Caroline head inside her condo building with a pep in their step, because they know Mortimer will have a plan to fix everything. They kiss sweetly and hug tightly before walking into the elevator. Dave pushes the button for the 29th floor. Dave and Caroline are so in love. Really hones in on how pathetic our love lives are. We can take solace in the fact we will never have what they have. Our lives are empty and nothing matters.

"DING!" chimes the elevator, alerting to our lovebirds that they've reached the 85th floor.

Stepping out onto the 346th floor, they race each other to Caroline's condo. Dave beats Caroline to the door because men are naturally faster than women.

"Haha! My legs have greater facets of speed than yours!" jokes Dave.

Caroline agrees.

"Meow," Cheddar meows timely, hoping this indie author distracted the reader and they've forgotten about the misogynist thing he wrote about men being naturally faster than women.

"Whoa! You look dishevelled, Cheddar. Are you okay?" Dave asks.

Cheddar meows sadly, pointing defeatedly at his door.

"Alright, well, stay fresh, my dude." Dave gives him two thumbs up, signalling with much enthusiasm that he indeed wants Cheddar to stay fresh.

Cheddar pulls out a baggy of catnip and starts rolling a sad joint, looking irrefutably miserable.

Dave laughs at Cheddar's drug addiction. "That looks like some pretty potent catnip, buddy."

"Meow," meows Cheddar, shaking morosely, wanting his fix so he can forget how depressed he is as the people do.

Caroline kisses Dave on the cheek. "I can't wait to hear Mortimer's amazing plan to get rid of Brenda and Business. It will be so nice when they're gone, and we can finally focus on you seeing what I look like below my navel." Caroline grabs her keys and unlocks her door, walks inside and is instantly mortified. Her entire condo is trashed. Every inch of the place — vandalized. She turns around towards Mortimer's fishbowl, and she breaks out into hysterics. "DAVE! DAVE! COME HERE! RIGHT NOW!"

Dave runs in, and opens his mouth to talk; smoke billows

out of his mouth between dry coughs. Dave's complexion turns green. Struggling to compose himself amongst the newfound mess and Caroline's dramatics, Dave leans against a wall of Caroline's open-concept living room. "That was not catnip," gags Dave.

"Are you okay? How's Cheddar," worries Caroline.

"MRRRRRRREEEEOOOOOOWWWWRRRR…"

Dave looks at Caroline wistfully… I think that's the word I'm thinking of. Anyway… Dave looks at Caroline wistfully, "Oh, he's having a great time as you can hear," chuckles Dave.

Caroline goes to the hallway on the 42nd floor and sees Cheddar flat on his back, spastically biting his tail, his back legs splayed in a way that you know damn well would get Brenda all hot and bothered.

"Cheddar, you're funny," giggles Caroline. She heads back to her living room and continues where she left off with her believable Academy Award-winning overdramatics. "Mortimer is gone! What could have happened to him? Who would do this?" Caroline shouts, her hands clutching the front of her dress in theatrical fashion, hoping the reader buys into her compelling performance. It worked. The reader is invested. Caroline achieved her goal.

Then Dave sees it – a piece of paper where Mortimer's bowl used to be. Dave picks it up. It's a note. Dave carefully drags his index finger across the letters, examining their texture, then pulls it to his nose and gives the note a sniff and an insurance whiff. Dave's eyes bulge from his face, "I know who wrote this. This was written with a 2H pencil. This note was written by only one business. It was Business. Business and Bren…"

"What does the note say?" Caroline rudely interrupting Dave from his Sherlock Holmes-level crime-solving epiphany.

"da took Mortimer," Dave finishing his sentence, agitated, side-eyeing Caroline, refusing to have his Where In The World Is Carmen Sandiego moment stolen from him. He then kisses her softly. His way of forgiving her. Dave grabs Caroline's hands and determinedly peels back her fingers so Caroline lets go of her dress where her boobs are. "That's enough, dear; the scene is over. This is a satirical romance, not some low-budget underdog Sundance Festival-nominated dramedy. Let's move on. It's time for laughs."

Caroline laughs.

"That's better," confirms Dave. Dave begins to read the note aloud, *"We have Mortimer,"* the note reads. "I knew it was them," Dave exercising his best Batman voice. "What would they want with him though? He's just a goldfish."

"Maybe they know that he's good at plans and are planning to use one of his plans so they can plan on killing us with one of his amazing plans," suggests Caroline after letting Dave finish his sentence this time because romance is like that.

"This isn't good. Such evil shouldn't have such power. We have to get him back, but where could they be?" Dave then sees a small arrow at the bottom right of the note, pointing to the right. Dave turns his head to the right and there against another wall of Caroline's open-concept living room was another note. He walks over to it curiously. It reads, *"We're across the hall."* Dave drops the note looking like he's just seen a dead ghost.

"What's wrong, my love? What is it?" Caroline's curiosity burning for answers.

Stuttering, Dave stutters, "Bren... Brenda... and... and... Bus... Bus... Business are back... back... at Bren... Bren... Brenda's con... condo."

Caroline doesn't like hearing that so she copies Dave and looks like she's just seen a ghost too. Caroline then puts on her angry face, stomps to her hallway on the 58thrd floor, steps over Cheddar, kicks Brenda's door as hard as she can and screams from the top of her lungs, "YOU'LL NEVER SEE WHAT I LOOK LIKE BELOW MY NAVEL EVER AGAIN! NOW GIVE ME BACK MY FUCKING GOLDFISH, BITCH! HIS NAME IS MORTIMER!"

Dave picks up Cheddar and gives him all the pets.

Brenda slowly opens the door, the chain restricting the door from opening up to its full potential. "Go away, Caroline. Business and I are plotting Dave's demise. Mortimer is so helpful. He has so many amazing plans."

Brenda then turns her posterior to the gap of the door, tightens every muscle in her body and coaxes out a most toxic fume from her breeding gland. As the violet cloud floats towards Dave and Caroline, paint from the hallway walls on the 37th floor begins peeling; the hazardous cloud growing stronger as it consumes their egg-white colour. Brenda laughs as Dave runs back into Caroline's condo with Cheddar. Cheddar is having a fucking day. Caroline shrugs disinterested. She's lived with Brenda for three years. She's used to it. The trick is to breathe through your mouth.

Caroline walks calmly back to her place, but not before yelling to Mortimer, "Don't worry! Dave and I are coming for you. Hang in there! We love you!" Caroline does her world-class hair flip.

There's powerful magic in her hair flips. Whenever she does a hair flip, any lice in her hair manifests into colourful butterflies. She does flamboyant hair flips to stay on top of her grooming regimen. Unfortunately, with Brenda's gas cloud still looming, all the butterflies die excruciatingly in Brenda's rectal gas. Again, to clarify, also the place where she breeds. No. Let's change that. All the butterflies lose their colour and turn into moths. Their brain chemistry changes. Their eyes fixate on the hallway's ceiling lights. Their new pilgrimage takes shape. Some way, somehow, they must find a way to get inside their glass casings so they can get trapped and die horrifically like their ancestors before them. Caroline walks into her condo and shuts the door.

"Meow?"

"Yes, you live with us now, Cheddar," Caroline giving him a big petty wetty on Cheddar's fluffy head.

The act of compassion pleases Cheddar. However, he can't help but imagine, wonder what life would be like if Brenda would just fucking die already. He really wants his stellar cat palace back. He's got some ladies coming over on the weekend because of how handsome he is. Cheddar gives Caroline a headbutt and one of his world-famous purrs. Staring longingly back where Brenda is still alive, he curls up his floofy paw and with his best Liiam Neeson impersonation meows, "Meow," shaking his adorable fist at her, vowing vengeance – a John Wick level of ass kicking.

Cheddar than bites Caroline's hand. Caroline approves of Cheddar's violent response. After all, she knows she broke the sacred three-pet rule. Cheddar jumps, plunks down knowing he successfully established his dominance and trots proudly to the bathroom because of how tough he is. But not the main floor bathroom. He went to Caroline's personal bathroom. Everyone knows bathrooms on the second floor are fancier than bathrooms on the first floor. How does Cheddar know Caroline has her own bathroom without ever being at her place before? Well, my friends, that's what we call in the literary industry – a plot hole. Cheddar then hops onto the edge of the tub and makes himself a hot bath. Cheddar has people abilities because Cheddar is fucking amazing.

Cheddar then sees a bag of Epsom salts sitting in the corner. "Meow," Cheddar reading the label. Perfect. It's lavender. Cheddar loves lavender. Swatting the bag three times – fap, fap, fap, fap, fap, he knocks the entire bag into the bath, because Cheddar has had a fucking day. Cheddar is happy, but something is missing. He looks around and there he sees her. Cheddar's eyes open wide with excitement. It's just what he needs.

"Meow," Cheddar meows.

"Porcelain by Moby from Spotify," confirms Alexa.

Cheddar jumps up on the counter and dims the light to set the relaxing mood. Cheddar is the happiest right now. Cheddar sees fresh towels hanging up. He's relieved. Cheddar doesn't know where Caroline keeps her towels. From the counter, Cheddar leans forward, his poofer butt wagging back and forth, his tail swishing, readying to leap, cannonballing his way into absolute fucking bliss.

Soaring into the air like a cat jumping from one place to another, Cheddar readies for the big splash…

"SPLASH!" torrents the tub water.

Cheddar leans back against the tub and rests.

"What the hell is going on up there?" Caroline wonders.

"I don't know," replies Dave. "Maybe Cheddar is having a hot bath. He has had a fucking day you know."

"You're right. He deserves it," acknowledges Caroline.

"So, what do you want to do now?" Dave asks.

Caroline playfully, wistfully walks up to Dave, whimsically gripping his tie, spinning it around her index finger, her other hand grasping his. "I have an idea," she smirks.

"And that is?" Dave acting clueless like he doesn't know Caroline wants to show him what she looks like below her navel, but he knows; he plays along with her because romance is like that.

As Caroline presses her body close against his, kissing him with all the passion in the world, Caroline guides Dave's hand up her dress; he lets her. Caroline's breathing grows heavier, faster. She's waited thirty-six years for this moment, but just as Dave is about to pull down Caroline's Sex In The City underwear, Dave suddenly stops.

"What's wrong," pants Caroline, doing her damnedest not to lose her fucking shit, because at this point she's kind of over Dave being such a flake. She keeps her cool.

"Mortimer, remember?"

Caroline understands where Dave is coming from. I mean it's her goddamn goldfish.

"We'll save him, but there's nothing we can do. We need a plan first. We might as well explore our bodies, or at the very least pull my underwear off, lift my dress and take a quick peek so you can finally see what I look like below my navel."

Dave opens his mouth…

"FUCKING PLEASE, MAN!" Caroline interrupts Dave from saying shit she doesn't want to fucking hear right now.

Surprised by the risen decibel range of Caroline's words, Dave wipes her saliva from his face and kisses her. "As soon as we get Mortimer back. I miss him. And who knows what awful things they are doing to him. We can't be selfish with our time. Let's save Mortimer first and I promise as soon as we do, I'll see what you look like below your navel. I promise."

Caroline at this point is too fucking horny to understand Dave's logic, but she believes him, because whether she agrees or not romance is like that.

"Okay," pouts Caroline in a huff.

They reunite with a kiss and start figuring out how to get their best buddy back.

But what Dave and Caroline don't know is that Mortimer already has a plan in motion, and it's working. Brenda and Business have no idea who they are fucking with.

I'm sorry but before I end this chapter, I have to say this. Caroline, if you're reading this, I want you to know if I were Dave, I would have railed you so many times by now… in every way possible. With permission of course. Have to clarify that so insane women don't try and accuse me of glorifying rape or something. Women are powerful and scary. Anyway, I know I shouldn't say shit about my own MCs, but I think me and the majority of people reading this story can agree that Dave doesn't deserve you. Like perhaps maybe Brenda has a point. Don't get me wrong. She's a terrible person, but man, damn, the things I'd do to you. Just want you to know you are desired. Oh, and don't tell Dave I said that. I don't want him getting upset and wrecking the direction of the story. The last thing I need is Dave getting upset, going rogue and starting up another business. He's come so far. Thanks.

Sincerely, technically your dad. Actually, let's go with *your creator*. Yikes.

ORGASM AND THE HAM SANDWICH

Now that Dave and Caroline found Brenda and Business' secret headquarters… across the hall on the 26th floor, they can begin drawing up their plans to eliminate the threats of their love and live the rest of their days uninterrupted. This is good because if Caroline doesn't show Dave what she looks like below her navel soon, she's going to go insane. However, Dave and Caroline are missing a very important aspect of their planning abilities. They don't have Mortimer, because we all know by now Mortimer makes the best plans, but Dave and Caroline's love is strong; it will overcome. It has to. People like happy endings. God forbid the antagonists win. That's literary speak for *baddies*. Fortunately for our lovers, Dave has been in business his entire life which means he's smart. He knows exactly what to do. So sit back and prepare to be amazed by Dave's huge throbbing brain.

"How are we going to defeat Brenda and Business without Mortimer's superior planning abilities?" Caroline asks, unaware Dave is about to punch her in the face with the greatest plan ever. Dave smiles at her, knowing she has no idea he's about to gape her mouth with astonishment with his gigantic plan. He's about to test her gag reflex with his intelligence when she drops her jaw in awe with a super amazing plan of his own. He's going to give it. She's going to take it. Why? Because romance is like that.

Dave walks to Caroline's arts and crafts room. Yes, you didn't know it until now, but Caroline has an arts and crafts room because she loves doing arts and crafts. She has an Etsy store. Her earnings are modest if you're wondering. On her limited edition crafting table, Dave grabs a blank piece of paper and a blue ink pad, walks back to the living room and confidently says, "This is it. This is our answer. We just need one more thing."

Caroline strangely looks at Dave, perplexed. "I don't get it," perplexes Caroline.

"Wait. You will." Dave then with a pep in his step heads up towards Caroline's bedroom.

"Where are you going? What. Are. You. Doing?" Caroline letting out a cute giggle of sorts. There's something about Dave's enthusiasm that always makes her experience juvenile feelings.

As Dave makes his way to Caroline's bedroom, he can hear the angelic voice of Cristina Aguilera singing, "I am beautiful no matter what they say, words can't bring me down." Her heavenly voice interrupted with echoing intervals of "meows". Dave walks into Caroline's super fancy bathroom where Cheddar is singing his little heart out, using a shampoo bottle as a sparkling diamond-studded microphone. Yes, Caroline's bedroom has an attached bathroom because, of course, it does.

"Sorry to interrupt, Cheddar, but the world needs you." Before Cheddar can give Dave a scowling of a lifetime, Dave grabs Cheddar from the back of his neck, wraps him up in a Sex In The City towel and dries him off.

"The fucking audacity," Cheddar meows. Cheddar wiggles violently, trying to break free. Cheddar meows for security. He can't believe he's being kidnapped during his sold-out concert. He can't understand why his security isn't stopping this. Where were they? Did Dave bore them to death with business talk? Cheddar is concerned about where he's being taken. The louder he meows and tries to claw Dave's eyes out for destroying his big moment, the tighter Dave squeezes. There's not a thing Cheddar can do, for Cheddar is now a burrito. Cheddar begins to panic. He knows if he doesn't finish the concert the sea of refund demands will bankrupt his entire tour. Man, Cheddar's narcissistic imagination is vivid as fuck. By the time Dave gets to the top of the stairs, Cheddar has given up, accepting the death of his music career.

"Is that Cheddar?"

"Yes, it is. Doesn't he look so cute? He's the cutest baby I've ever seen." Dave then continues to bombard Cheddar's ears with irrefutable baby talk.

This annoys the shit out of Cheddar, but I'd be lying if I said he doesn't thrive on being complimented in rapid succession. Meanwhile, Caroline is basically soaking her Sex And The City panties. That baby talk is making her ovaries explode like a billion-dollar fireworks extravaganza. She needs Dave to put a baby inside her fucking yesterday with his male penis. Using all her willpower, Caroline quickly puts her vagina through a drought; she knows there are way bigger problems at hand. Once Brenda and Business are permanently removed from their lives, then she can focus on getting Dave to take a little peek down there and see what she looks like below her navel. Come Hell or high water, Caroline is going to be Dave's bottom.

As Dave makes his way down the stairs enthusiastically, he says to Caroline, "Are you ready to be wowed? Check this out." Approaching the ink pad, Dave carefully, gently unfurls Cheddar. Cheddar then sees an opportunity to claw some eyes out, escape. Realizing this, Dave asks Cheddar, "Do you want your condo back or not?" Cheddar stops, retracts his claws and reluctantly hangs his head in defeat.

"Meow," Cheddar meowing submissively.

"You can trust me, Cheddar." Dave then presses each one of Cheddar's paws on the blue ink pad and has him walk across the blank piece of paper.

"Oh my god, Dave, are those what I think they are?!"

"Yes, they're blueprints. They are legitimate plans."

"Mortimer would be so proud of you!"

"I figured he would be," Dave big-smiling a smiley smile of smiles. "Okay, so according to these blueprints, this is how the plan is going to go down."

"Meow." Cheddar cries tears of joy. Not only is he happy that he's about to get his condo back, but the beauty of his creation got him right in the feels. Cheddar no longer wants to be a music star. Cheddar wants to become an architect. Cheddar wants to be the best architect in the world. Cheddar also wants to run all over

Caroline's swank condo and leave blue paw prints everywhere, because even though Cheddar is happy, he's still beyond aggravated that Dave ruined his big concert. I mean what if Cheddar was in the middle of recording a platinum album? Studio time isn't cheap. Cheddar reestablishes his dominance by activating the zoomies. He knows Dave and Caroline at their core are way better people than Brenda, but lessons must be learned. Cheddar then begins running around the kitchen and living room – little blue pawprints dabbing everywhere behind him. Successfully letting it be known he's never to be manhandled like that again, Cheddar turns his head, hisses a mighty hiss at my main characters, and promptly heads back to the bathroom.

"That cat is so silly," Caroline doing her darndest to hold back laughter.

KER-SPLASH! "MEOW!" Cheddar's bathwater is cold. Cheddar angrily drains the tub and runs a new bath. Not like it's his water bill. Cheddar doesn't give a fuck. He's going to give the concert of a lifetime that his fans deserve. Cheddar forgot he wants to be an architect.

Dave and Caroline's eyes divert away from the sounds of Cheddar bitching and their eyes lock. Stuck in a love-locked gaze, their hearts palpitate not slowly, the temperature of their bodies increases with heat, and they kiss with the passion of an orgy taking place during the mighty Roman Empire because romance is like that. Caroline takes Dave's hand without consent and guides it up her dress. Closer and closer, Dave's fingers begin to tingle from the heat emitting from Caroline's pelvarian cavern. The drought is over. Their hormones charge at each other like jousting knights fighting over medieval kingdoms. Could this finally be it? Is Dave going to see what Caroline looks like below her navel? Is Caroline going to get steamrolled and have a gender baby? The attraction between them at this very moment is something they've never felt before. Shit be fucking heavy. Dave's shy fingers graze the tips of Caroline's pubic hair like in that Gladiator scene where Russel

Crowe walks through the field of tall grass. Or was it wheat? Either way, Caroline is ready to be taken, taken away to Elysium. But I'm not. The sex isn't happening yet because I want you to wait longer. Settle the fuck down, pervert. It's a beautiful romance story about two fictional characters in love, not a fucking screenshot of your spouse's infidelity on Whatsapp.

Dave snaps out of MDMA Cupid's trance and heroically face-palms Caroline with his nonperverted hand. "Stop. We have to stop," pants Dave like a breed of dog you've probably had as a pet when you were a kid. "The plan. We have to double focus on the plan."

That was it. Caroline goes apeshit. Grabbing Dave by his Snoopy tie, she pulls him in close and whispers a threat in a Cruella Deville tone into his ear. "Listen to me, David, and listen closely - if you don't at least put one finger inside me, I'm going to kill your entire family."

Dave is terrified. More importantly, confused. Dave's entire family was killed in a freak chuckwagon-cruise ship accident thirty-six years ago. Dave is stone-cold stunned at how Caroline could be so dark, and malicious, but worse, Dave is offended by how she could forget such an integral part of his life considering her parents suffered the same horrific fate. Then it hits Dave. Can Caroline be a supernatural being from a parallel universe who has a doctorate in necromancy? Is she going to resurrect his entire family only to butcher them in front of him? NAAAAAAAAAAAAAAAH… Dave is a Gemini which means Caroline is a Gemini. Dave solves the puzzle. She's acting out because she's hangry. Dave is so smart with his detective thoughts.

He puts his Caucasian hands on Caroline's Caucasian face, looks deep into her Jezebel-green eyes and says the thing every woman wants to hear their man say, "Honey, I'm going to make you a sandwich."

Caroline's hormonal rage instantly subsides, the red hue on her face deletes off her skin — the natural Caucasian-ness of her skin beiges before him. But before Dave can think about what kind of tasty ingredients he's going to use for the sandwich, Caroline's rested face precariously goes full Grinch. It's then she forcefully pushes Dave against the wall, gripping his wrist like an oversized, overly aggressive pinchy-pinchy Cancer crab, which is nuts because she's a Gemini. If anything I should have referenced a butterfly. Doesn't matter. She forces Dave's hand underneath her dress; his eyes opening so wide with fear, that they pop out of his head like 99 Luftballons Auf ihrem Weg zum Horizont.

"Do I look like I'm a fucking chastity mannequin? You're going to put a finger inside me whether you like it or not, and you better make me moist as a picnic towelette or I'm going to make it two fingers, then three, then four. We'll keep going until both of your fists are inside me if we have to. And why, why are you going to do it?"

"Be... be... because... romance is... is... like that?" stutters Dave with trepidation.

"Such a good boy I have. Now go ahead, I'm waiting."

Eventually, Dave is able to get his pinky finger erect enough to obey directions. Shyly, cautiously like a worm entering a section of soil it's never been in before, he penetrates his tea party finger up past Caroline's labia. "Bottom's up," Dave jokes to himself.

Caroline wraps her arms around the back of Dave's neck, moaning. Dave's pinky at this juncture is now all the way inside her. Caroline is leaking like a 1980s waterbed past its warranty – just gushing pasty secretion all over his hand. She then lifts her leg up against Dave's 34" waist, grinding hard into the little pinky that could. Dave grabs her leg for stability. He doesn't want Caroline falling over and getting hurt. Dave is so caring, so loving... Damn, Dave is hard. Something is happening to Dave. His body is going through changes he never felt before. There's a monster in his pants desperately trying to escape, but to Dave chivalry isn't dead. He knows this ravenous monster wants inside Caroline more than anything. He has to hold it back at all costs.

Then it happens. Caroline has one of those orgasm things and lets out the biggest "OH FUCK!" you've ever heard. She is satiated. She good. The sound of a cork gun firing confirms the removal of Dave's pinky. The amount of gooiness on his hand can alarm Ghostbusters. Dave hopes he's done enough to save his dead family. Caroline's eyes look up at Dave with satisfaction. Kissing him while mouthing the words, "Thank you," she gives Dave's lip a playful nibble and tells him to go make her that sandwich. Dave is relieved. Dave has done it. Dave indeed has saved his dead family from dying twice.

Heading to the kitchen of Caroline's open-concept condo, which means from the living room he can walk unobstructed into the kitchen without worrying about walking into any walls. Still confused and feeling slightly violated by what just happened, he begins to make Caroline a fingerbang sandwich... Sorry... make Caroline a sandwich. He grabs bread, mayonnaise, Monterey jack cheese and some sliced ham. Dave sets the first slice of bread on the counter, then with laser focus spreads mayonnaise on it. Dave has to make this perfect. After all, he's being a chef right now. That. And also, he's a tad worried what will happen if he doesn't make the greatest sandwich the world has ever seen. Caroline... Caroline... Phew... Humpf... Caroline might make him use his tongue next time. This is troublesome for Dave because everyone knows taste buds are strictly for food items only.

"How's that after-orgasm sandwich coming along?" asks Caroline sweetly.

Dave's hand shakes like a prized fighter with Parkinson's Disease as he sets the ham on the flattened mayonnaise, which is exquisitely situated on the bread. Oh. The bread? It's sourdough. No. Let's make it multigrain. "Goo-goo-good, my love. R-eady in a mo-moment." Dave is so fucking scared right now.

Then he sees it. The slight fold in the slice of ham sets off a cataclysmic chain reaction of tremors in his hand. His pinky finger curls, stiffens into his palm. The other four fingers try to console it, comfort it, that everything is okay – it's just ham. Three fingers and a thumb if you want to be a dick about it. It doesn't work. Pinky has seen things, felt things; the other pinky whispers to the other hand to get its shit together, worried about what will happen to it if Caroline doesn't get her sexual assault sandwich. Dave puts his hand in the business pocket of his business pants. It's useless. Pinky is officially a traumatized timid turtle. The other hand can't risk it. Putting on a cape, it's ready to be the hero of this deli. With authority, it slams down a slice of Monterey jack cheese, finalizing the construction with the second slice of peasant loaf bread. Yes, I changed the type of bread again. Not only that, but the other hand also added mustard to that second slice. Please understand ham sandwiches without mustard is criminal. Disagree? Okay, well, you're an idiot and I don't like you very much. I also added romaine lettuce. No. This isn't right. This estrogen-dictated sandwich isn't good enough. I'm changing it to a soft brioche bun. Fuck, Caroline keeps a lot of bread. She is rich, so when it comes to the storyline this makes sense. The sandwich is complete. The cape is red.

"How's that eatable sandwich coming along," asks Caroline sweetly."

"At max potential. I'm bringing it towards you now."

"Great. I am famished."

Dave walks into the living room of Caroline's open-concept condo. Flying the ham sandwich around like a superhero. Caroline laughs as Dave hums catchy superhero music as he wooshes and swooshes it about. WHAT A GUY! WHAT A SANDWICH! WHAT A FUCKING ENTRANCE! Dave locks in. With expert precision he swoops and zooms that ham sandwich to Caroline's mouth; the ham sandwich accepts its fate to be viciously broken down by a slathery horde of enzymes. Caroline opens her mouth. No blow job fascinations strike Dave's thoughts. Me, however… Anyway, Caroline takes a big bite.

"AAAAAAAAAHHHHHH!" The ham sandwich screams

in agony.

"What the hell was that?" Caroline with her mouth full of something that's unfortunately not my penis.

"No idea." Dave is relieved that the ham sandwich seemed to have calmed Caroline's toxic feminity the fuck down.

Now that the ham sandwich is dead and Caroline is back to her darling self, Dave is ready to lay out the plan to Caroline and get Mortimer back before that bitch Brenda and Business can use Mortimer's superior planning abilities to permanently fuck shit up for them. Dave grabs Caroline's hand and walks her to the blueprints that will lead them to victory.

"Your hand is sticky," accuses Caroline. "And why is there white stuff on it? It's flaking off. What is that? Did you not wash your hands after taking me to Ecstasy Village?"

Dave stops and looks at her with so much love, so much forgiveness for violating his pinky finger, "Yes, sanitization is what hearts adore and I bloody adore you," he confesses. "It's probably just handruff. It's like dandruff but of the hands."

"Oh, okay," replies Caroline in a trustworthy tone.

Dave, however, lied; he did not wash his hands. He forgot, but he isn't going to tell her that she possibly ate some of her own secretion, because romance is like that and maybe fear. Honestly, probably mostly fear. I mean, do you blame him? We're all kind of learning there's more to Caroline than we first thought. Let's just forget any of that happened and go back to believing Caroline is a sweetheart, not a sex-crazed monster. God, I wish someone would Calgary Rodeo my pinky. Sigh. Fuck, I'm lonely. Okay, fine – and pathetic. Happy now?

Dave kisses Caroline on the cheek because she has remnants of ham sandwich on the corners of her mouth. Not one of her sexiest moments. I'd still tap that though. Sorry, sorry, I've seemed to be sexually attracted to my own MC. Hey, remember when I said I was lonely and pathetic? Let's continue with the story before one of my hands finds its way down my pants. What am I even doing with my life? Sigh.

"So, this is what we are going to do." Dave placidly gestures his noncontaminated hand over the blueprints of his foolproof plan and begins to tell Caroline how it's going to go down.

Caroline jumps up and down with excitement. "There's no way this plan can fail" Dave doesn't realize the hypnotic wiggle of Caroline's boobs from her enthusiastic hopping. But I sure did.

"You ready to get our fish back?" says Dave in a protagonist full of optimism sort of way.

"YES!" Caroline is happier than she's been in ages.

Dave does a fist pump. "Let's go then!"

Caroline also does a fist pump. "Yay!"

Dave and Caroline walk through her open-concept condo towards the front door. She doesn't have a back door, well, she does, but I'm not going there. Her condo doesn't have a back door because condos don't have yards. Okay, yes, they have doors to their balcony, but that doesn't count. No, fake grass so people's dogs have somewhere to shit isn't a yard. It's a balcony soul patch at best. Frankly, if people are too lazy to take their dog outside for a walk, so they can do puppy business, then they shouldn't own a fucking dog. Fight me. Listen, who fucking cares. Caroline doesn't even have a dog. She has a goldfish. Let it go. Why are you arguing with me? I'm trying to tell you an epic love tale. Ugh, why are you like this?

Dave gentlemanly opens the door and escorts Caroline out, because ladies first. Dave is such a gentleman. Sometimes I feel like Caroline doesn't deserve him. I deserve her though. All of her. I need therapy or an orgasm that doesn't involve the pinky finger of a sexually inept man.

Stepping into the carpeted hallway of the 94th floor, Dave and Caroline promptly walk roughly three steps to Brenda's door. Business is in there with her. They're as ready as they'll ever be. They're getting Mortimer back.

Should Dave and Caroline enter Brenda's condo and catch

Brenda contracting lead poisoning because Business is HBouncing itself into her ass? Yes? No? Hmm… I'll think about it.

OUT OF BUSINESS

"Knock, knock," the door knocks as Caroline's Caucasian knuckles thud against Brenda's door. Caroline glances over to Dave who is standing off to the side, so Brenda can't see how sneaky he's being. Caroline is nervous, but Dave takes her fears away with a gratuitous thumbs up. Dave has belief thoughts in her. She's got this.

Brenda presses one of her bulbous eyes against the peephole and sees Caroline standing with her arms tightly at her side, smiling inconspicuously. "What do you want, Caroline?" garfs Brenda.

"Hi, it's me, Caroline. Can you open the door and leave yourself vulnerable for a moment so we can talk and not hit you with a surprise attack from Dave?"

Dave instantly gives Caroline not one, but two gratuitous thumbs up, showing her she's doing a great job so far. Through her peripherals, she confirms that Dave supports her lying abilities. She smiles.

"Why are you smiling?" derps Brenda.

"That's what I want to talk to you about. I murdered Dave with a cheese grater while he was sleeping. My heart couldn't bear the ouch feelings of not being with you anymore," falsely confesses Caroline.

"Really? Prove it."

Caroline cues intensely dramatic music in her head and in slow motion holds up a bloody cheese grater.

"Oh, my god! I knew you loved me more than him, every boil on my skin knew it!" Brenda opens the door like a troglodyte with a weakness for door-to-door salesmen. Saleswomen if you're a sensitive sexist. "Business, come here, you have to see this!"

Wobbling over to Brenda, because remember Business has pencils for arms and legs. "What is it? Has my white-out shipment arrived? I NEEEEEEEEED TO GET HIIIIIIIIIIIGH."

"Nope, even better."

"Oh, it's Caroline. What do you want, homewrecker?"

"Look! Look! Look at what she did! She grated Dave's face with that cheese grater like a waitress at a fancy restaurant!"

"Okay, settle down, baby beluga in the deep blue sea, don't get your flubber melted down into an oil lamp."

Brenda and Business are having relationship issues, but it's Brenda so I get it. Business is conflicted. Yes, it's happy Dave died a horrific death but is also disappointed it'll never get the chance to kill him with lead poisoning.

"Cool," Business acting like it didn't care vengeance wasn't theirs.

Brenda interrupts Business' regretful writing utensil feelings with disgusting excitement farts. Business scowls at her just fucking annoyed about her entire existence. Without a doubt, these two are the worst assembly of evil villains and lovers that ever cohabitated.

Suddenly, Caroline does her best Undertaker impression, rolls her eyes in the back of her head and drags her tongue across the cheese grater. Is it me or is Caroline kind of insane? Sure, she's sweet and her overall demeanour and poise give the sense that her whistling could bring all the woodland creatures to her yard. Well, she doesn't have a yard, so maybe the balcony of her condo on the 66th floor. To be honest, she scares me a little. Don't get me wrong, I'd definitely tap that, but my guard would be up. I'd hate to get on her bad side and find myself chopped up and shoved into a garbage bag filled with rocks — my dismembered body crashing a mermaid surprise party as it sinks to the bottom of the ocean. Talk about awkwardness. But damn, I bet she's so tight. Yeah, I'd risk it. One million percent. What the fuck is wrong with me? I need help.

"What, what, what is happening?" Brenda snurbles.

"I'm kind of getting this feeling I should've stayed at Dave's office and continued living my best life in the Samurai Pizza Cats pencil case. There were snacks in there."

Business is right to think that way because what they don't know is, that the blood and skin on the cheese grater is shredded cookie dough and red food colouring. Dave and Caroline's plan is working. Then Business' mouth opens in shock. There's Dave, standing in front of it after hiding alongside the wall by the door for a considerable amount of time.

"Hello, Jacob Marley; consider yourself Scrooged," Dave dropping the second coldest line in literary history.

"It's a trap!" Business shouting the obvious.

Dave then punts it across Brenda's living room, revealing that her condo is far from an open concept, or maybe it is, but it's hard to tell with so much stuff piled up everywhere. Hoarders are like that. Business crashes hard into a soiled pile of 80s Playboy magazines.

Brenda's eyes immediately cross from the plot development and nervously shits herself.

Caroline stares at Brenda's defecation, then looks up at her, smirks and says, "Congratulations, it's a boy," swiftly kicking her in the face with a classic Patrick Swayze Road House kick. Brenda falls backwards, rolling, crashing into her pink inflatable couch like an obese villain who everyone hates; whoever reading this cheering, relieved they're finally getting their money's worth from buying this God-awful book.

The commotion wakes up Mortimer from a cool dream. "Blub blub blub?" confused on what's happening. It's then he looks over and sees Dave and Caroline strutting into the living room like Double Dragon, before getting into their perspective battle stances. Caroline is badass. Dave is relatively the same. The scene of them together about to fight evil side by side is epic.

"Blub! Blub!" Oh, my god, it's Dave! Dave is here! And Caroline too. Mortimer is so happy to see his dad. Jumping in and out of his fishbowl.

Dave turns to him with the soul and spirit of every character Jason Statham has ever played and gives Mortimer the world's biggest affirming thumbs up. Mortimer is ecstatic, pumped up. He does a quick twirl in his bowl, before getting himself to a vertical base to show off his lightning-fast Shaofin Monkfish maneuvers. Mortimer is ready to battle alongside Dave 'til death, but he can't because if he left his bowl he would asphyxiate and die. Fish need water to breathe. Gills are like that. Mortimer knows that so he just does some fin punches and wicked tail kicks, establishing how lucky Brenda and Business are that he's confined to a small space.

Brenda and Business regroup and make a charge at Dave and Caroline like they're anime characters no one gives a shit about.

Brenda tackles Caroline against her LG refrigerator. She bought it on sale at Best Buy. She then immediately tries to gore her beautiful face with her walrus tusks. Caroline bobs and weaves her head, avoiding the impact of Brenda's Animal Planet instincts.

Meanwhile Business screams, "ITSY BITSY! ITSY BITSY TRANSFORM!" Business drops to all four pencil tips and runs up Dave's blue business slacks with the rage of a meth-addicted spider, stabbing him as it makes its way up Dave's chest.

Covered in tiny punctures, Dave falls to his knees; the blood loss from Business' lethal attacks minimal at best. Dave reties his shoelaces, rips Business off his chest and throws Business into an open pantry closet. Business crashes into Cheddar's old litter box, disrupting the biggest cockroach orgy you can possibly imagine. Not sure why Brenda would keep a litter box in the same place where you store food, but I think it's well-established that Brenda is fucking gross and does gross things. Like she's been back in that condo for what — a few hours and she's already turned the place into Oscar the Grouch's summer vacation home. Man, killing her off is going to feel so good. Oh, sorry — spoiler alert.

Let's observe how Caroline and Brenda are doing. HOLY SHIT! Caroline hit Brenda with a hurricarana! Brenda is getting her ass kicked! I can't wait to write more on what happens next.

Sitting on the floor, dazed, and weakened, Brenda wipes off some random purple goo off her mouth; her mandibles pinching in frustration. "Is that all you got?" arrogantly stamping her two front hooves on the floor.

Glinting her eyes in a way that would make Clint Eastwood jealous, "No," informing Brenda that she indeed has more to give.

"I do not want to do this, baby doll, but you leave me no choice." Brenda beast punches through her Doritos cupboard and as dozens of rats scurry out, Brenda pulls out one she crushed. Hooves are like that.

Caroline isn't aware, but Brenda is about to power up. Her mandibles shred the dead Splinter as they shove it into Brenda's gullet, Brenda begins to stand formidable, squeaking high-pitched notes of doom! Caroline stands in fear as she watches the front of Brenda's neck open up, revealing an esophageal chasm of rat teeth. She wants Caroline's cheese and she wants it now. Ha! Brenda is a Maximal.

"B... Brenda? Brenda? Are you feeling fresh, top-notch?" Caroline concerned about what she just witnessed. Rightfully so.

"Never better. I have transformed," drools Brenda rabidly, demonically glaring at her. "NOW GIVE ME THAT PUSSY!"

Her neck's mutated rodent mouth gnaws wildly at her as she charges somewhat full tilt at Caroline because she only has one foot. She leaps on top of her, knocking her to the kitchen's pink linoleum floor. This is impressive considering how huge Brenda is: 534lbs and having the vertical leap of Tigger despite looking like she's devoured the entire Hundred Acre Wood is something not many can do.

"Dave! Help me! She wants my pussy! Help me!" Caroline screaming, trying to hold back Brenda, stop her from doing... Ugh, I'm going to vomit. Let's just end it here. I can't stomach this shit anymore.

Dave stands up because he finished retying his shoelaces, but before he can say positive and heroic words to her, Business crawls out of the pantry covered in cat shit. No one is surprised Brenda has never cleaned out Cheddar's litter box.

"You think you can destroy me, David? I am you and you are me. If I die, you die. MUAHAHAHAHAHA! Prepare for murder-suicide. If I can't have you no one will." Business then does this cool jumping super spin attack at Dave like a ninja throwing star. What Business should've realized though since they are ONE, is that Dave really hates being called David. Dave isn't scared. He dials in and is about to do something radical. If you keep reading you'll see the gangsta thing he's going to pull off.

"DIIIIIIIIIIIIIIIIIIIIIIIIIIIIIIIIIIIE!" Business screeches as it twirls at supersonic speeds, aiming for Dave's head.

Knowing that Caroline's thirty-six-year-old pussy is under threat of being munched into oblivion by Brenda's newest feeding hole, Dave moves at the speed of quantum ultra-light, dodging Business' super secret power spinning move, catching it with ease in the process.

"HOW IS THIS POSSIBLE?!" Business demanding the origins of Dave's clear use of witchcraft.

Dave smirks at Business and says, "Let's just say I never miss a deadline." He then swiftly throws it at Brenda, and right before Brenda can get a taste of Caroline's sweet nectar, one of Business' legs pierces through Brenda's neck, puncturing a fartery. A fartery? A fartery is one of Brenda's crucial lifelines I've never mentioned before. It supports her central nervous system and is practically an instakill when damaged. Neat eh?

Brenda reels back, reacting similarly to when the Gnome King from Disney's *Return To Oz* eats a hen's egg for the first time. "Wha... wha... what have you done?"

"Okay, that's it. I'm done. I'm going back to my Samurai Pizza Cats pencil case. Fuck this shit. I'm out." Business trying to pull its leg out of Brenda's fartery.

"You think you can stop me?" Brenda rips Business out of her neck and throws it away.

"PLUNK," goes the tepid water in Mortimer's fishbowl, as Business falls in.

Brenda gags, belches; blood and gas come pouring out of her neck. Her scaley skin shrivels. Teeth from her mouths fall out. Her organs eviscerate. And then like a striking asteroid that doesn't know how to ask for directions, Brenda shoots across her landfill. Whether she likes it or not, Brenda is justly going out like a sad party water balloon.

"Do you think she's in any pain," asks Caroline as Dave picks her up off Brenda's pink linoleum floor.

"Honestly, I don't know. How can anyone know?"

"AAAAAGGGGHHHHH! I'M IN SO MUCH PAIN!" hollers Brenda as her body crashes into the bathroom, exploding on impact against the open toilet seat. Deflated animal parts are everywhere. This is fitting, because not only is she a terrible person, but she's also a terrible character.

Holding Dave's nose for dear life, knowing he isn't immune to Brenda's foul odours, they walk together through the green gas plume and head towards the bathroom, to check and see if Brenda's alright. Entering the bathroom they can hear something sloshing around inside the uncleaned toilet. Dave waves his hand to push away Brenda's fartery gas. Dave and Caroline look down, horrified at what they've stumbled on. In the toilet is a purple blob about the size of one of my testicles that don't work, because vasectomies are like that.

"That is different looking," states Dave.

Caroline throws up.

"I neeeeeeeeeed tooooo feeeeeeeeeeed!" screeches purple blob Brenda.

Dave wastes no time and executes a precise Tae Kwon Do axe kick and flushes the toilet with the heel of his foot. And fuck me, is Caroline super impressed. Don't think she hasn't forgotten about getting Dave to see what she looks like below her navel. It's not just about feeling it; he needs to LOOK at it.

The purple blob formerly known as Brenda is successfully flushed where she will live out the rest of her days in the town's sewer system as a snapping turtle's oral stress ball.

Dave and Caroline hug in celebration and kiss in a way you'd think a timely fireworks display would appear above them, but like everything in my life, this story doesn't have the budget for that. So they kiss and nothing happens.

Dave chuckles, "Let's go get our goldfish back."

"Yeah, sure, let's do that." Caroline a little annoyed Dave abruptly stopped their moment like that for a goldfish, they both damn well know is alive and well.

Caroline walks in front of Dave with agitated feelings. Dave follows closely behind her, unaware she's being a sensitive bitch about it, but romance is like that. Man, Dave can't wait to give Mortimer a thumbs up. Two even.

Back in the kitchen Business is still alive, because I forgot to kill it off. Barely clinging to the edge of Mortimer's fishbowl, Business tries to pull itself out. Business is scared. Business also can't swim. Business without question is dealing with a plethora of issues like terror and a lack of functional fingers.

Business sees Dave and begs for forgiveness. "Dave! Dave! Partner! I'm sorry! Help me, please! If you help me I promise to leave your life forever and finally let you see what Caroline looks like below her navel!"

Before Dave can reply, Business is fiercely pulled down into the unfiltered water. Mortimer is pissed. Mortimer has had enough of Business' shit and wrecking his family. Mortimer wants blood. Mortimer fiercely grabs Business where a pencil's neck would be and pushes it to the bottom of his bowl, choking it, blubbing so many fucking obscenities at Business. Essentially, Mortimer is telling Business to swallow a fat mermaid's dick and die.

As the last air bubble leaves Business' mouth, which is weird because pencils don't have lungs, Mortimer swims to the surface to greet his dad. I suppose he's also glad Caroline is there too.

"You did good, little buddy." And that's when Dave hits Mortimer with the best thumbs up he's ever given to anyone.

Mortimer leaps out of the algae-infested water… Fuck me, Brenda's place did a real number on Mortimer's water quality, didn't it? Where was I? Oh yes… Mortimer high-fives Dave's thumb with his tail, doing a midair somersault on the way down.

"SPLASH!" reacts the water to Mortimer's aerobatic entry.

"Let's get you home, champ." Dave picks up the fishbowl. Mortimer is so happy.

"Oops, not you," Caroline plucking Business' dead body floating facedown out of the water and throwing it back into Cheddar's litter box, once again disrupting the cockroach orgy.

"Nice shot, hun," compliments Dave on her casual use of accuracy.

"Thanks, love."

Holding Mortimer in one hand and Caroline's hand in his other, the reunited family walks out of Brenda's pigsty and into Caroline's open-concept condo across the hall on the 970th floor.

BLUB

At the white marble island of Caroline's kitchen inside her open-concept condo, Dave holds up Mortimer's fishbowl in the air, the sunlight through the window majestically glistening the stagnant water like Dave is worshipping a Greek god. Mortimer flexes his fins as he basks in the glory because Greek gods are like that. Dave is proud of Mortimer. Caroline is proud of Mortimer too. Truthfully, Mortimer doesn't give a shit how Caroline feels now Dave is back in the picture. Don't get him wrong. Mortimer does love Caroline, but come on – this is Dave we're talking about. Can you blame him? Man, look at Mortimer's muscles. No wonder Business didn't stand a chance. Damn Mortimer, you single?

"How you holding up, Zeus?" Dave makes Mortimer blush, setting him down on that white marble island of Caroline's kitchen I mentioned earlier. Fuck Rockefeller money. I want Caroline's money. I should write in this story how she goes bankrupt and loses everything because, at this point, I'm just mad and extremely jealous. Okay, and yes, pathetic. But that's already been established.

"Blub, blub," Mortimer blowing bashful bubbles because he adores how much Dave cares about him.

"I'm happy you're alright, my strong guy," Dave patting Mortimer on the head with his index finger, because it's his longest finger for some reason. "Did Brenda and Business at least treat you with fish respect while they held you captive?"

Mortimer takes a deep breath, "Blub blub blub blub blub blub; blub blub blub blub. Blub blub blub blub blub blub blub. Blub blub blub. Blub, blub, blub, blub, blub blub blub blub. Blub blub blub blub blub blub blub blub blub blub blub blub blub blub, blub! Blub blub blub blub blub; blub blub blub blub blub blub blub blub blub blub. Blub blub blub? Blub. Blub blub blub blub blub. Blub blub, blub blub blub blub blub blub."

"That is horrifying. I can't believe you were able to endure all of that. I don't think I could handle that level of abuse. Admit it, you are a Greek god, aren't you? Come on, you can tell me," boasts Dave, making Mortimer feel so fucking special. Mortimer blushes. Can you blame him? Wish Dave was my dad. And other reasons why life isn't fair. "Did they do that to you too?" Dave pointing at tasty BBQ grill sear marks on Mortimer's left side.

"BLUB! BLUB! BLUB BLUB BLUB BLUB BLUB! Blub, blub blub blub blub blub blub blub blub, blub blub blub blub. Blub blub blub blub blub blub, blub blub blub blub blub! BLUB! BLUB! Blub blub blub! Blub blub blub blub; blub blub blub blub blub blub blub blub blub blub, blub!" goes Mortimer in precise detail on how Brenda and Business threatened to make a Highliner fish stick out of him if he didn't create a foolproof plan to dispose of Dave and Caroline. Well, mostly Dave.

Dave seeing Mortimer grilled to near perfection showed him how much Mortimer loves his family. There's no fucking way Mortimer was going to tell them shit. Says a lot, because if I were Mortimer, Dave and Caroline would be mulched in the wood chips of a playground. Not only am I pathetic I'm also a coward. Speaks volumes about my character that I envy a goldfish, doesn't it?

Caroline goes to the cupboard and grabs a jar of Vasoline for Mortimer's Gordon Ramsay's George Foreman Grill marks. Caroline is not a nurse. Mortimer waves her off. He doesn't need to be lubricated. He's too tough for whatever the fuck Caroline thinks she's doing. Caroline wide-eyed is in disbelief Mortimer doesn't need the healing powers of Vasoline. She gives him a smile. Mortimer rolls his eyes and looks back at Dave's ocean-blue eyes. Now that's a body of water Mortimer can see himself in. He sees a lot of himself in Dave. That's why Mortimer loves him so much. Or he's just fish gay in love with him. I'm not going further into that rabbit hole. There's a good chance none of us will ever come back from it. Let's stick with platonic love grown from admiration and respect, shall we? No one needs vivid imagery of an insatiable horny goldfish getting sodomized by a full-grown man, or worse, a full-grown man getting sodomized by an overly frisky goldfish with endless determination. Although...

"Did it hurt being grilled to perfection?" politely asks Dave, and timely as to distract the reader from how closely we've avoided an entire chapter about fantastical scenarios of bestiality.

The reader stares intently at their thrift store garbage can, contemplating if continuing on with the story is worth it... Their curiosity prevails. The reader comes to terms with the possibility they're a fucking pervert. This may be a hard truth for them, but they're okay with it because after they finish the book, they're going to log on to their Amazon account where all of Liian Varus' books are available for purchase and leave a one-star review on Romance Is Like That even though, they've probably masturbated seventeen times throughout this book. Lord knows I have. Feeling called out, the reader puts their pants back on and begins reading again to find out if being grilled to perfection gave Mortimer ouchy feelings.

Mortimer puts on a tough face, "Blub blub blub blub blub. Blub, blub blub blub blub blub blub blub blub blub. Blub blub blub blub blub! Blub, blub! Blub blub blub blub blub blub blub blub blub blub. Blub blub blub blub; blub blub blub blub blub blub. Blub blub blub - blub blub blub blub blub blub blub, blub blub blub blub."

Dave can't believe how Mortimer endured that. Aspiring to be as strong as Mortimer one day, he gives Mortimer another pat on his head with his eerily long index finger; very reminiscent of ET if he were giving a goldfish some petty wetties. So cute. In the background, Caroline goes through the refrigerator, searching to see what condiments can be used as topical ointments. Dave peers behind him, because Caroline's senseless rummaging is interrupting Mortimer and Dave's special moment.

"Caroline, my love."

"Yes," Caroline standing up, holding a bottle of mustard.

"Put the mustard back."

Giggling, Caroline realizes she's being a little silly, "Sorry,

I'm realizing I'm being a little silly." Caroline puts the mustard down and stands beside Dave, giving Mortimer a gentle wave.

Mortimer breathes a sigh of stupidity on behalf of Caroline.

"Mortimer, can I ask you something gross? I don't really want to know but curiosity is getting the better of me."

"Blub blub, Blub, blub blub blub," acknowledging Dave. Dave composes himself before asking the question no one needs an answer to. "Did Brenda and Business have sex with each other?"

Mortimer is confused as to why anyone would want to know this, but Dave is his dad. Mortimer loves Dave so of course he is going to tell him.

"Blub blub blub blub blub blub. Blub, blub blub blub blub blub blub, blub blub blub blub blub blub blub - blub blub blub blub blub blub blub. Blub, blub blub blub blub blub blub blub blub blub blub. Blub blub blub blub blub blub, blub blub blub blub blub blub blub blub blub blub blub blub. Blub blub blub. Blub blub blub blub blub blub blub blub blub blub blub blub. Blub blub blub blub blub; blub blub blub blub blub blub. Blub blub blub blub blub blub blub blub blub blub blub blub blub blub blub blub blub blub blub. Blub, Blub blub blub blub, blub blub blub blub blub blub blub. Blub blub, blub blub blub blub blub blub blub blub blub blub blub blub? Blub blub blub blub blub blub blub blub. Blub blub blub blub blub blub blub blub blub. Blub blub blub blub blub blub blub blub blub blub blub blub blub; blub blub blub blub blub blub, blub blub blub blub blub.

Dave and Caroline glance at each other, turning a swampy green, doing their best not to projectile vomit their disgusted feelings from the horrors Mortimer gave in vile detail. Dave and Caroline look back at Mortimer, his eyes bulging with shock and trauma. Clearly, Mortimer has seen things he will never be able to unsee.

"Poor guy," Dave using the powers of empathy to show Mortimer he's empathetic of what he's gone through. Caroline is also empathetic. Mortimer appreciates it, but Dave's empathy is enough. He doesn't tell Caroline this, because he doesn't want to give her embarrassed feelings. After all, Mortimer does love his mom; he truly does, but again, this is Dave we're talking about. Dave's the coolest.

"Mortimer," Dave trying to get Mortimer's attention and pull him out of the dark abyss he's trapped in. "MORTIMER! MORTIMER!"

"Dave, it's not working. We're losing him! Do something!" Caroline shouting the obvious scenario Dave is quite aware of.

Luckily Dave is standing because he always thinks quick on his feet. "I have an idea. It's a tad bit unorthodox but possibly crazy enough to work."

"Do it! Whatever it is, do it!"

Dave then takes both hands to the sides of his mouth and reenacts gills as he puckers his lips. It works. Mortimer laughs, coming back to reality, forgetting the different ways Business gave Brenda 2Herpes.

"Blub Blub, blub blub blub blub blub." Mortimer putting his fins together in a prayer-like fashion, showing appreciation to Dave for rescuing him from a mental nightmare.

"You're welcome, handsome. Glad to have you back."

Caroline inexplicably intervenes in Dave and Mortimer's special moment. Not on purpose, but sometimes Caroline needs to learn how to read the room, "So now Brenda and Business are defeated, what do you guys want to do?" abruptly turning around to pick up the bottle of mustard off the counter. Why? I don't know. Maybe she just likes the way it feels in her hands. Is it that farfetched that some women love the feeling of hard, thick things in their hands? At this point, why do any of my characters do any of the things they do? Caroline yearns precociously about wanting the mustard to splurt out and accidentally shoot all over her face. See? See what I mean? Great. Now I have to try and finish this book without my writing abilities being inhibited because I can't stop wishing my dick is a mustard bottle. Kidding. I don't have any writing abilities. Caroline puts the Heinz mustard bottle back in the fridge, because of everything I've written so far, it makes the most sense. Yes, the mustard is Heinz.

Mortimer takes a minute and comes up with the perfect idea to celebrate their victory. Acting like an adorable puppy good at swimming, enthusiastically he raises a fin.

"Whoa, settle down, boy. Yes, what's your idea, buddy?" Dave happily acknowledging Mortimer's excitement.

Mortimer then points to the freezer, "Blub blub Blub, blub blub blub blub blub blub blub! Blub blub blub blub blub blub blub blub blub blub blub blub blub blub blub blub blub blub blub! Blub! Blub! Blub! Blub blub blub blub blub blub blub blub blub blub; blub blub blub blub blub blub blub blub blub! Blub blub blub blub blub blub, blub blub blub blub blub blub blub blub blub!"

"What do you think, sugar pill? Shall we make Mortimer's dream come true?"

"Of course, are they even dreams if they don't come true immediately?" Caroline keeps strong eye contact with Dave, failing terribly at sounding prophetic.

"Blub?" Mortimer struggling with why she couldn't have just said yes, but happy all the same.

Dave goes to the freezer and pulls out a half-empty tub of triple hot nut shot fantasy chocolate fudge ice cream. Caroline only bought it a few days ago, but she can't help herself. She loves the way a load of triple hot nut shot melts in her mouth, basting her tongue with its array of sweet, nutty flavours. Caroline drools a little, thinking about how many spoonfuls she took last time – her mouth consistently filled to the brim. She swallowed a lot of loads that day. I'm betting she can at least take one more. I'm ready.

Grabbing some maraschino cherries, caramel syrup and whipped cream, Dave makes Mortimer the best sundae the world has ever seen. Mortimer's eyes light up, burning brighter than at least two, no, three suns. He can't wait. Meanwhile, Caroline tries to hide how wet she is and how mad she is at herself for allowing Mortimer to eat the rest of her favourite ice cream, but then she remembers how rich she is, realizing she can just get a new tub of triple hot nut shot fantasy chocolate fudge ice cream later. Caroline is no longer mad. Still wet though.

"Go ahead, Mortimer. Jump in," encourages Dave in an encouraging tone.

Mortimer rockets out of his fishbowl fifty feet in the air. If you ask him. Realistically it was about five centimeters. Mortimer lands in the tub of triple hot nut shot fantasy chocolate fudge ice cream. Immediately Mortimer activates his fish lips and ravenously begins puckering at the amazing flavours the triple hot nut shot fantasy chocolate fudge ice cream provides. His body convulsing from its heavenly taste, coating his body with its divine texture as he slips and slides inside the tub like an Olympic snowboarder asphyxiating to death on a halfpipe. If Mortimer wanted to die, it is here, now. Mortimer nibbles at the maraschino cherries, dabs his cute fishy tongue against the drizzle of caramel, and then does the most amazing thing – Mortimer dabs whipped cream onto his head and where a human chin would be, giving himself an afro and a bushy beard, and pretends to paint a gorgeous mountain scene while portraying an untouchable impersonation of Bob Ross. Dave and Caroline laugh so loud. It one hundred percent confirms how incredibly funny Mortimer is. Caroline more than anyone needs the distraction because she's been standing there with drenched panties, soaking herself like SpongeBob.

"Okay Mortimer, that's enough," Dave seeing Mortimer about to die from being out of the water too long. "Hope you got your fill. You deserve it." Dave then picks up Mortimer… Oops, Dave drops him. He tries again. Drops him. Picks him up even gentler this time. Drops him again. Over and over, Mortimer's almost lifeless body falls back into the tub of triple hot nut shot fantasy chocolate fudge ice cream. Dave has stressful feelings. If he can't get Mortimer back into his fishbowl soon he's going to die.

Dave then finds calm. He problem-solves. He knows exactly what to do. Dave quickly gets a salad fork and goes to jab it into his side. This way he knows there will be no way for Mortimer to slip out of his hands. The salad fork comes crashing down like King Neptune's trident... And then BAM! It hits him. Dave stops shy from Mortimer's dessert-coated grilled to perfection side. This will kill him! Dave immediately drops the fork, grabs the little fish net and scoops Mortimer up instead, putting him safely and very much alive back into his fishbowl.

"Blub, blub blub blub blub blub blub blub blub!" Mortimer thanks Dave for saving his life. Mortimer gives Dave a thumbs up, confirming he indeed is well. Well enough for seconds.

"No, no, no, my aquatic friend, I think you've had enough," Dave politely shattering any chance of Mortimer's dream having a successful sequel.

"Blub." Mortimer understands Dave's logic. Understands, but is sad as fuck though.

Dave sees the sadness lambasting itself all over Mortimer's facial expressions, he picks up a maraschino cherry and drops it into Mortimer's fishbowl. "Here you go, my man."

Mortimer's eyes illuminate brighter than at least five more suns and immediately starts pressing his fishy lips against it, taking a piece, nibble by adorable nibble. If this isn't fish paradise then I don't know what is.

"Where are you going, sweetie C?" Dave noticing Caroline waddling awkwardly to the stairs with her legs crossed in a peculiar self-containing way.

"Oh, um, I just need to do something."

"Alright, well, don't be long. You're going to miss out on Mortimer eating this maraschino cherry."

Caroline's sexy body vibrates. "OH GOD!" Screaming out the direness of her situation she frantically runs up the stairs, rushes through her bedroom and passes a snoozing Cheddar who by far is having the best spa day and flails herself towards the bathroom.

Thankfully Cheddar forgot to drain the bathwater. She jumps in and instantly executes any existence of her vagina's sexy feelings.

"What the hell was that about?" asks Dave, perplexed.

"Blub blub blub blub blub blub blub blub blub," Mortimer giving his two cents intermittently between maraschino bites.

"Do… Do you think I should follow her?" Dave knowing exactly what he risks walking into, but knows it's time.

Mortimer swims to the edge of his fishbowl and hits Dave with a reality check – the greatest inspirational speech of all time. "Blub blub blub blub blub blub blub, Blub. Blub blub blub blub blub blub blub blub, blub blub blub blub, blub blub blub blub blub blub blub - blub blub blub blub, Blub. Blub blub blub blub blub blub blub blub blub blub blub blub blub blub blub blub blub, blub blub blub blub blub blub blub blub blub blub blub blub blub blub blub blub blub. Blub, Blub, Blub, blub blub blub blub blub blub blub blub blub; blub blub blub blub blub blub blub blub blub blub blub blub blub blub! Blub, blub blub blub blub blub blub? Blub blub blub blub blub blub blub blub blub blub blub blub blub blub blub blub, blub blub blub, Blub? Blub blub blub blub blub blub, blub blub blub blub blub blub blub blub, blub blub blub. Blub blub blub blub blub blub blub blub blub blub! Blub, blub blub blub blub blub blub blub blub blub blub blub blub blub blub blub blub blub blub blub, blub blub blub blub blub blub blub blub blub blub blub blub blub blub blub blub blub blub blub blub blub. Blub blub blub blub blub blub blub blub blub blub blub blub blub blub blub blub blub blub blub blub. Blub blub blub blub blub blub, blub blub blub blub blub? Blub blub blub blub; blub blub blub blub blub blub, Blub. Blub blub blub blub blub blub blub blub blub! Blub, blub blub blub blub blub blub blub blub. Blub. Blub. Blub, blub blub blub blub blub blub blub! BLUB! BLUB! BLUB! BLUB! BLUB! BLUB!" From the look of determination encased over Dave's blue eyes, Mortimer knows Dave is ready, brave enough to give Caroline multiple orgasms via a myriad of sexual positions.

"You're the best, buddy." Dave marches confidently up the stairs; his hormones leading the way to the bedroom where some sex is definitely going to happen.

Mortimer goes back to eating his maraschino cherry.

As Dave walks into the bedroom, he sees Cheddar napping, sprawled out peacefully on his back; having kitty dreams for sure. "Hey, sleepy head, time to wake up," gently waking Cheddar by caressing his belly.

Cheddar reluctantly opens his eyes; perturbed by Dave's intrusion, he bites him viciously on the hand. Cheddar's dream of being a cotton candy astronaut was over. Cheddar isn't fucking thrilled with Dave. Not at all. But Dave goes on to tell Cheddar that he, Caroline, and Mortimer murdered Brenda and Business in cold blood and now he can move back into his condo. Cheddar is so excited about this, he leaves the room quickly and without apologizing to Dave for biting him on the hand, because Cheddar doesn't apologize for shit. But in his own way, he is thankful for Dave, Caroline and Mortimer for helping him piece his life back together because appreciation is like that.

"I really should get that cat a maid," Dave remembering the absolute shit show condition that condo is in.

"Dave?" Caroline noticing Dave standing by her bed.

"Yes, I'm Dave," says Dave.

"What are you doing in here?"

"Let's just say a little goldfish told me you wanted to show me what you look like below your navel."

"Oh?" Caroline bites her lip seductively.

Dave moves towards Caroline's vicinity like a chauvinistic male following strict guidelines of moral etiquette. I'm not entirely sure what that looks like, but because Dave doesn't have steroid muscles, he doesn't come off as threatening and it's effectively warming Caroline's vagina like an electric heating pad. Whatever it is he's doing, Caroline feels safe, secure and doesn't regret leaving her phone with the Sex And The City case downstairs because she isn't being draped and overwhelmed by wave after wave of red flags. Dave is being a man, taking control of the situation. Caroline knows she's about to get pounded and she is ready for it. Honestly, I'm proud of Dave for taking the initiative. I would never despite my sexual attraction to Caroline. Hell, I'm even too scared to touch my own wife. Well, ex-wife. Same difference. Fuck. Wish I had a goldfish to inspire me not to be a pathetic piece of shit. Alas… Dave firmly wraps his arm around Caroline's mouth and kisses her passionately on the waist. Er, sorry… Dave firmly wraps his arm around Caroline's waist and kisses her passionately on the mouth. Caroline fucking swoons as she drenches herself; Dave is about to open those floodgates.

THE SEX

"I'VE WAITED A LONG TIME FOR THIS, DAVE."

"I know. Me too. I'm sorry you waited a long time for this Caroline."

"How bad do you want me?" Caroline leans back against the footboard of her bed, being hot as fuck.

Gradually his palms warm up like a McDonald's heat lamp.

"Do you want me?"

"Yes."

"Prove it. Make me want you like a jungle cat with birthing hips," demands Caroline.

Ooooo, she's playing hard to get. I like that. It's good for the story to have an increase of sexual tension before the inevitable clanging of genital jousting. I'm so good at romance, it's scary.

Dave knows it's the least he can do even though he's the least suave guy in the world. Unable to come up with smooth sexy moves, Dave begins to panic. He's about to blow it. He can't afford to let Caroline down. He needs to do something, and just as hope seems lost, he comes up with a plan – rapid-fire pick-up lines. He smiles. He's fucking got this.

"You're smiling, that's a positive sign," says Caroline.

Dave winks. "Hope you are prepared for those butterflies in your vagina's stomach to start fluttering in rapid-fire succession. Are you ready?"

"Give it to me, Dave. GIVE IT TO ME!" pleas Caroline.

"Damn girl, are you a live studio audience? Because I want you to give me the clap."

Caroline portrays a bewildered face, truthfully an insulted one. Hell, I'd be confused too. "Dave, hunny, if you want this," pointing at her vagina like a Basset Hound tracking down a fox, "then you're going to have to do way better than that."

"You're right," Dave acknowledging how fucking terrible

he is at this. Dave takes a moment to come up with something to redeem himself… … … … … … He's got it. A decent entry-level pick-up line. Dave goes for it and says, "Just call me Pat Benatar because I'm about to hit you with my best shot."

Caroline's smile levels up to her ears, confirming to Dave he's on the right track. "You're getting it, sweetheart. Keep going. You're on the right track."

Dave's eyes squiggle down before looking up at Caroline, knowing he's about to make her heart drop some sick beats. Before Caroline can say another word, Dave attacks her with a sentence created with words made up of sexy syllables, "Are you a record, because I'm about to set you straight."

Caroline instantly remembers her relationship with Brenda and all the disgusting things Brenda and she did with each other's bodies. Putting her hand over her mouth, barely keeping the rising vomit at bay, gagging, she tells Dave to stop. Right off the bat, Caroline taps out.

What Caroline doesn't know is that Dave has come too far and waited too long for this moment to end. He tries again anyway. "I know I came inside your house, but I'd rather come inside you."

Caroline's eyes open; her breasts perk with interest.

"Oh my god, it's working," Dave says to himself, hyping up for the next banger line. "Hey girl, want to hibernate? We can fall asleep together while IT's still inside you."

Caroline's female blood temperature rises upwards because it's getting warm. The hair on her arms starts standing like worms coming out of the soil for the first time. Alerted by the heat tide of bubbling hormones, the vomit recedes to its starting point.

"Tell me more, hunk," licking her lips.

"I'm no vegetarian, but I'll toss your salad." Dave tries to keep it cool because even that line surprised him. Caroline tries to keep it cool too, but the steam coming out of her ears isn't hiding anything. This kettle wants to scream. She's getting too hot. Dave isn't done. He wants to bring Caroline to a boil. "Hey baby, how do you like your pork? Because I like mine pulled."

Caroline's jaw drops. Fighting every urge to skip the hand job and go right into the blow job. "Ugh," moaning softly. "More. Give me more," she begs.

"Did you lose something? Well, maybe you should go find me attractive then." But what Dave doesn't know is that Caroline already finds him attractive, but just not attractive, she finds him hot as fuck. Girl's skin is sweating beads for him. Dave isn't done yet, he remembers Caroline's most favourite eye activity – reading, and goes with an absolute stunner of a line, "How about we take your love of reading and start a book club… but it's Eyes Wide Shut?"

Caroline almost loses it, gripping the footboard with her hands. Weak knees from a powerful surge of estrogen impede her balance; she wants Dave's D bad, and I don't mean the first letter of his name.

"You must be a skydiver because baby you're falling so fast I know you want to yank my cord." Dave waves over his penis like it's the Price Is Right Showcase Showdown. And it's working. Caroline wants to be the big winner.

By the way Caroline is salivating he knows oral is on her mind. As Caroline's drool falls to the floor, Dave has no doubts – his flirting game is the best in the world.

"Oh, Dave! Dave! Convince me to take my floral dress off!" Caroline upping the decibels of her desire so Dave knows what her desire is.

Dave steps directly in front of Caroline, because this whole time he's been talking to her at some weird offputting angle like an extra in a movie that's accidentally getting too much screen time. He clutches the front of her dress just above her boobies, and continues the flirtatious assault with this dynamite line, "You must be a skydiver because baby you're falling so fast I know you want to yank my cord."

Wait. I already wrote that. Meh.

Caroline vulture-clutches the footboard harder, imagining Dave has two penises so she can extract double the amount of his man milk. That's *semen* for you, lactose-intolerant folks. "Dave, I can barely contain myself," Caroline thrusting her obvious birthing hips at him.

Dave methodically drags his finger guns across her soft lips like a melted popsicle, reassuring her there are more words to come. Instantly precipitating, Caroline is bombarded with hot flashes of hormonal imagery. She can no longer take it, but Dave isn't done yet.

"Hold on. I'm not done." See? Told you he wasn't done. Dave then blows Caroline away with this seasonal banger. "We must be reindeer, because Cupid has me wanting to Comet to you, Vixen."

That's it, Caroline rips her dress off. In her beige bra and underwear, Dave does a double take, because he thinks Caroline is naked. Beige is like that. "Take me, Dave! TAKE ME NOW!"

Dave firmly presses his hand against her chest, "Not yet. I want you dripping for me. Be my leaky faucet."

Caroline uncrosses her shaven legs, so Dave can see exactly when her vagina turns into a natural-occurring geyser, "Okay. Go. Drip me like it's hot."

"Damn girl, if you are a ray of sunshine, then I must be a garden because you're making my peony erect," giving Caroline a cool guy wink. Dave then inspects her entire body with eyes and says in a Sherlock Holmes voice, "Hm, seems as though your limbs are attached entirely to the wrong body."

Absolutely beside herself, she's ready to pounce. Caroline wants nothing more than to be Dave's misgendered Watson, then Dave says something that pushes Caroline over the edge. "Are you a hemiplegic migraine? Because you're making my head throb."

Unable to pronounce the word 'willpower' she grabs a hold of Dave's peony, and immediately realizes she is a ray of sunshine, because Dave's peony without question is erect, "Mmm, I can't wait until this blooms inside me."

Realizing the intensity of their intending intense intensity of their sexual wantings, Dave decides to ease up on the tension with poorly-timed humour, "Damn girl, are you AI-generated? Because you're touching me with a hand that shouldn't be there."

Caroline laughs. Slightly offended, but womanly laughter overcomes the unnecessary awkwardness Dave lays on her. She understands how hot and heavy things are getting and doesn't want Dave blowing his load prematurely, because she's attached to a hungry vagina that needs feeding; like Hell, she's going to let go of her python grip. This dick is fucking hers.

"Caroline, are you a mechanic? Because you are doing an amazing job at tightening my nuts. Here. Let me help you loosen them," unbuckling his belt because romance is like that. Dave removes Caroline's dick-grabbing hand and says, "Just call me The Truth because I'm about to expose myself." Dave's business pants experience gravity, falling to its scientific whims, revealing his He-Man underwear; He-Man's face bulgier than usual.

"Oh my," Caroline gasps, staring at Dave's fully erect penis barely held back by the power of nature. Her hands spring into action. Gripping the waistband of Dave's super cool underwear, she seductively pulls them down. Dave appreciates the freedom she gives him.

Dave's breathing intensifies because he's horny. The line is crossed. The sex is going to definitely happen… eventually.

"Are you speed dial? Because I only want to touch you once and then have you do the rest of the work," Dave not letting up on his assault on the femininity of her moist genitals.

Caroline shouts at the top of her lungs, "GOD! YES! I AM SPEED DIAL! TOUCH ME!"

With a mighty poke from his even mightier index finger, he presses Caroline's forehead, imagining there is an elevator button on it. Caroline melts. She's never felt so good; her body invigorated by his Midas touch, she falls to her knees and takes a firm grip on

Dave's pelvarian sausage. She's ready. He's ready. Caroline wants a mouthful.

Snatching Caroline's hair like a crow stealing a robin's egg, he pulls on it and says, "Giving me a blow job might not make me be more in love with you, but it's a head start," in his perfected Elvis voice. Dave is so amazing at impersonations. The eagerness of Caroline's ever-gaping mouth is enticing the shit out of Dave right now.

"Damn girl, you must be a circus seal, because I want to bounce my balls off your nose."

Before Caroline can adjust her face to appease Dave's new desire, Dave surprises her with an oral penis poke. Like a flying bug flying into a spider's web, Caroline speedily snags Dave's cock with both hands as her lips lock on tight, making sure it can't escape the pressure of her squeezing tonsils. Caroline has one goal and that's to bruise the shit out of her uvula. With her Iron Man grasp on Dave's penis, she pulls it further into her mouth; her uvula begging for mercy as she wraps her tongue around Dave's beige submarine like Venom eating a Subway sandwich.

Moaning reminiscent of a dubstep song no one gives a shit about, Dave knows now that some holes in fact do get all the glory. Feeling like a teenager volcano, he knows if Caroline keeps going, she's going to choke on his white-hot magma, and god forbid it goes down the wrong pipe. Spicing up their sex life by putting cumin her is the correct way to do things. Dave didn't come this far to play toothpaste dispenser. He wants the hole that matters.

"GAG! GUG! GIG! GEG! GYG! GOG!" Caroline makes the necessary sounds to tell the reader she's sucking Dave off with much enthusiasm.

Suddenly a bra strap slips down off her shoulder and lands in her elbow's armpit. Dave looks down and sees her Natural Geographic booby exposed to the elements. "Damn girl, are you the Himalayas? Because your Nepal is showing," approving of her boob-to-nipple ratio. Caroline sucks this dude's dick harder. The fucking suction on this girl, I tell you. Fucking wow.

"GAG! GUG! GIG! GEG! GYG! GOG! GAG! GUG! GIG! GEG! GYG! GOG! GAG! GUG! GIG! GEG! GYG! GOG! GAG! GUG! GIG! GEG! GYG! GOG! GAG! GUG! GIG! GEG! GYG! GOG! GAG! GUG! GIG! GEG! GYG! GOG! GAG! GUG! GIG! GEG! GYG! GOG! GAG! GUG! GIG! GEG! GYG! GOG! GAG! GUG! GIG! GEG! GYG! GOG! GAG! GUG! GIG! GEG! GYG! GOG! GAG! GUG! GIG! GEG! GYG! GOG!" Caroline continuing to enjoy Dave's Godzilla dick in her thirsty mouth and without even smearing her lipstick. Fuck. I'll be back. I... um... have to do... something...

Okay, back. Where was I? Oh yes... Dave pulls his dick out of Caroline's mouth at cheetah speed, because he's about to puff out Caroline's cheeks like a hamster stealing food at a party it wasn't invited to. Cum. He's going to cum in her mouth for those not familiar with analogies.

"That's enough, that's enough," Dave panting like a happy dog that just got back from a good 5K run. He picks Caroline up off her knees and kisses her in a way that makes her abscess over him. Caroline goes breathless. Fuck, she loves this man so much.

Caroline stares deep into Dave's blue eyes, her arms around his neck, holding herself up because her wobbly knees are sore from pressing against the hardwood floor for so long, "Look down, my love."

Dave points his eyes downward as Caroline asks, without manners mind you. Anyway, Dave's eyes sparkle at the sight of a huge puddle on the floor; reminiscent of an African desert watering hole. Noticing how drenched Caroline's underwear is, he knows it is time. He knows exactly what time it is. "Get. On. The. Bed," Dave taking control of the sexuation.

"Caroline goes weak, "Yes, daddy."

"My name is Dave," sternly correcting her, throwing her on the bed like one of King Kong's barrels.

Caroline then lies down, head on a pillow, knees up, legs together and calls Dave over with a slight bend of her finger. Dave in a manly way takes off the rest of his suit, which is good because he's been wearing the same suit for like three years, and for the sake of not ruining the sex scene, we're also going to forget that he also hasn't showered in that amount of time as well. And yes, this whole time Dave has had a ZZ Top beard. No, it is realistic. This is what happens when you ignore personal hygiene because you're too focused on business. Can we please, please get back to the amazing sex scene that's about to happen? Thank you.

Dave gets on the bed, kneeling in front of Caroline's feet. Noticing their shadows on the wall, Dave begins to make her even wetter like that's even possible at this point. He takes his fingers and starts finger-gunning her shadow's vagina. Pewing her again and again.

"Oh fuck!" moans Caroline's shadow.

It's at this moment he knows he has her. Picking up a shiny pair of conveniently placed scissors, Dave takes hold of Caroline's beige panties and carefully cuts them up like a paper snowflake. He's done it. He gains access and proceeds to kiss Caroline like a male, slowly dragging his tongue from her lips, down her neck, her chest, across her breasts and down the middle of her stomach. His tongue moves sluggishly like a slug crawling across a campsite, slower and slower as the salt content of Caroline's sweaty skin impedes the mechanics of Dave's slithering tongue because slugs are like that. Finally arriving, barely, Dave primes up Caroline's hormones like a pair of Reebok Pumps by pressing all her right buttons with the best examples of foreshadowing in history.

"Damn girl, are you a paper straw? Because I want to put my mouth on you until you're soaked and useless. Times like this I wish my tongue was pierced so you and I could play Ring Toss with your NuvaRing. Your pussy may look like a groundhog but I'm still going to gopher you. AU, I might not be Australian, but I'm about to go down under. Fuck, I must be vegan because I want to eat you and then tell all my friends about it."

Before Caroline can confirm she is indeed not a paper straw, doesn't have a NuvaRing inserted, tell him the name of her pelvis' groundhog, give him citizenship to her genitals or remind him he doesn't have a social life, Dave begins tracing Caroline's G-spot with the tip of his tongue. Caroline loves it, not giving a shit why it feels like he's writing the letter Z. She knows if he licks long enough through the alphabet, he'll eventually get to the letter G.

"Oh, oh, oh, oh, oh... OH!" Caroline's body writhing in pure ecstasy.

This is Dave's first time having Caroline for lunch. Her pussy is meatier than expected but knows Caroline believes in him. He's up for the fellatio challenge awaiting him. "SLARP! SLURP! SLIRP! SLERP! SLYRP!" Dave flaunting that his suction also has game. Making sure not to be shellfish, Dave sucks Caroline's clit like inhaling an oyster at a fancy seafood restaurant. See? Told you he's up for the challenge.

"More! More! More!" Caroline moans, gripping her retro Golden Girls comforter tightly as Dave shucks her pussy.

With perfect choreography, Dave's fingers dance into the scene, his fingernails tiptoeing, mesmerizing like oversized ballet slippers; walking across her labia like Yellowpages, he finds the business he's searching for. The reader claps their hands in awe.

"This is everything zen," moans Caroline.

The tongue strokes longer, slower, W-I-D-E-R, as Dave proves he's an even bigger bush fan. Dave bites off the nails of his index and middle fingers, so as not to accidentally Jack The Ripper Caroline's insides, and then hurriedly scurries them into Caroline's vagina like a timid spider.

Surprised by Dave's new tactic, Caroline bursts her squirts all over Dave's face, "FFFFFFUUUUUUCCCCCCCKKKKK!"

Dave continues shoving as many of his body parts in her as possible; unphased he wasn't wearing his glasses when blasted. As he wriggled his fingers inside, he could tell Caroline is thankful her vagina is ambidextrous. Dave's penis is gyrating; he knows if he can keep up this amazing performance their sex will come to fruition.

Wiping off Caroline's homemade secretion her body made, the scent of her body's pheromones makes him crazy, animalistic, one hundred percent Jumanji. The fragrance is good, ever-wafting; his penis stiffens at the thought that soon it will smell just like her. But Dave knows he has to work, swoon even harder to convince Caroline's legs to do long division, but he is up for it. After all, he has a Master's in Business — sexy time business. He lays it on thick. There's no time to waste.

"Excuse me, ma'am, but are you a chip? Because you look Frito Lay."

Caroline's eyes well up, the sadness of knowing she isn't a crunchy, salty chip puts her emotions into a full-blown crisis. "I'm not," cries Caroline. "I hope it's okay, but I understand if it's not."

"Don't be silly, Caroline," says Dave, "I'm just being silly. How about I tattoo *SPIRITS* on your legs so I can lift them?"

Caroline laughs, understanding that Dave doesn't care if she isn't a crunchy, salty chip. "You can't tattoo me, but you can lift my legs." Caroline is confident that Dave will love the feeling of her recently shaved legs against his skin.

Dave grabs Caroline's ankles and slowly lifts her legs over her shoulders like a Boeing 747's landing gear. Her eyes open as big as airplane windows. The climax gaining altitude.

"Please! Please! Talk dirty to me!" Caroline begs, as her pussy reaches for Dave's cock, trying to achieve symbiosis.

Dave doesn't hold back. He lets her have it, "Hey girl, are you into taxidermy? Because I'm going to stuff you until you're stiff. I might not be familiar with birds, but I know how to spread an eagle. Are you a fitted sheet? Because I'm going to fold you in so many different ways until it's good enough because I don't know what I'm doing. How about I write *SUNRISE* and *SUNSET* on your legs and I expand your horizons? Damn girl, you must be clouds, because I want to put my head in you. I may be in crippling debt, but I'd rather be in you. Damn girl, are you an old staircase? Because you look like you need a good railing."

As Caroline lies sweating like a 1980s aerobics instructor, exhausted, vulnerable, hypnotized by Dave's magnificent use of sexy language, he transports her entire being into the Heavens of Pleasure with the greatest panty-remover line ever said by anyone, "Can I call you Paillard? Because I want to pound you raw."

"AAAAGGGHHHHH!" Caroline moans louder than I did watching scrambled porn as a teenager in the 90s. That's it. Caroline is fucking done. She grabs Dave's very hard penis because boners are like that and sticks it inside her because romance is like that. It's an indescribable feeling. They see fireworks. Dave quickly pulls out, gets up and closes the curtains. The outside fireworks are too distracting.

"That's better," says Dave as he slides his juicy cock back into Caroline's starving vagina.

Now as someone who isn't really experienced with sex or how people really are, I'm not going to get into details about the whole sex thing. I imagine there's a lot of in, out, in, out, and both are having the time of their lives. Overall, I would say it probably feels pretty good for both of them.

Uh oh... Dave leans back, afraid, "You... Y... You're bleeding!" stuttering, fearful he just committed manslaughter.

Caroline looks down and comforts Dave. "Congratulations hunny, you did it! You've obliterated my hymen. Yay!"

Relieved he is not the reincarnation of Jack The Ripper, and not having any clue on what the fuck a hymen is, Dave in a Biblical voice bellows, "Just call me Moses, because I'm about to part your Red Sea."

With Caroline's leg hooked, Dave leans in and just goes to absolute town on Caroline's special place of interest – moaning, kissing, genitals banging hard against each other, making squelchy sounds – blood everywhere.

Dave then gets a sexy idea. "Hey Caroline, do you want to

play Zoo? I'll be a sheep, you be a donkey, and I'll ram your ass."

No hesitation, Caroline turns around and lifts her ass in the air like a stray cat in heat, caterwauling down a dark alley, "FUCK MY ASS, DAVE! FUCK IT!" Caroline pleading to be torn wide open.

Dave wasting no time takes his swivel-headed penis and augers it deep inside her rectum, until he finds the lost gremlin world of Froglim. Kidding. I have no idea why I wrote that. Dave fucks Caroline's ass with his normal-shaped human cock. Dave is thankful Caroline is good at wiping. Dave's penis begins tingling in a certain way; something neat is happening. He then remembers something about his grade 8 sex ed class. His penis is about to vomit white Oreo cream stuff - his own special marshmallow paste. Interrupting all the sounds of the animal kingdom that Caroline is making so he can inform her of the potential cum shots her ass is about to receive, he asks, "Want to know how a failed vasectomy works?"

"YES! YES! MY TARZAN MAN! MAKE MY APE GO SHIT!"

Dave with complete control asks, "Want to know why nice guys finish last? Because they let their women cum first."

He then gives her the hardest thrust and BOOM! Caroline has the biggest orgasm any woman has ever experienced. So hot. Caroline exhausted by all the steamy passion collapses in a heap of sweaty body parts, panting like a dog back from a 5K run. But Dave isn't done.

"You must be a bowl of popcorn because when I'm done, there's only going to be seeds left in you." Turning her over onto her back, he spreads her legs as wide as they can go and puts his cock deep past where Caroline's hymen used to be and fills her with at least two gallons of semen. Or so it feels. Dave's entire body pulsates, dumping loads and loads of microscopic penal worms inside her. The amount of sperm injected inside her is countless.

Dave might not be much of a baker, but he guy can certainly cream a pie. Dave collapses alongside Caroline; they kiss each other sweetly because romance is like that. They had such a great time fucking. Personally, I'm jealous. Also pathetically pathetic. But mostly jealous. Dave gently leans into Caroline's ear and says, "Are you Backgammon? Because I'll never play you."

"Yahtzee," sighs Caroline happily.

"I promise I'll never hurt you again, because believe it or not, babe, I'm the man of your mildest dreams. I have to ask you though, are you a foundation? Because your face looks like it could support a building."

Caroline blushes. Dave isn't perfect, but he always has the cutest ways when telling her how beautiful she is. Then he says what Caroline has been waiting for her entire life. Pressing his lips to her ear he completes her, "I love you more than business."

It's at that moment Caroline knows Dave loves her more than business. Caroline means the entire world to Dave. She deserves to know how he truly feels. After all, she's his first hug, first kiss, first date, first girlfriend, first love, first sexual partner, but more importantly, she's his first cousin.

THE END.